Fourth Grade Fairy

Eileen Cook

Aladdin

New York London Toronto Sydney

This book is a work of fiction. Any references to historical events, real people, or real locales are used fictitiously. Other names, characters, places, and incidents are the product of the author's imagination, and any resemblance to actual events or locales or persons, living or dead, is entirely coincidental.

ALADDIN

An imprint of Simon & Schuster Children's Publishing Division

1230 Avenue of the Americas, New York, NY 10020

First Aladdin paperback edition April 2011

Copyright © 2011 by Eileen Cook

All rights reserved, including the right of reproduction in whole or in part in any form.

ALADDIN is a trademark of Simon & Schuster, Inc., and related logo is a registered trademark of Simon & Schuster, Inc.

For information about special discounts for bulk purchases, please contact Simon & Schuster Special Sales at 1-866-506-1949 or business@simonandschuster.com.

The Simon & Schuster Speakers Bureau can bring authors to your live event. For more information or to book an event contact the Simon & Schuster Speakers Bureau at 1-866-248-3049 or visit our website at www.simonspeakers.com.

Designed by Jessica Handelman and Karina Granda

The text of this book was set in Lomba.

Manufactured in the United States of America 0311 OFF

2 4 6 8 10 9 7 5 3 1

Library of Congress Control Number 2010019963

ISBN 978-1-4169-9811-2

ISBN 978-1-4169-9814-3 (eBook)

Acknowledgments

This book wouldn't have been written without the awesome help of Kaiti Caul and Molly Sullivan, two of the coolest girls on the planet. Thanks for helping me understand fourth grade and not making fun of me when I got it all wrong.

Books don't get made without the input of a lot of people. Thanks to Rachel Vater and Emily Lawrence, who made a good book even better. As always, thanks go to my family and friends for putting up with me during the process.

Lastly, thanks to you for picking this book! I hope you have as much fun reading it as I did writing it.

one

Why having an older sister is a pain:
- She never lets you touch her stuff.
- She bosses you around all the time.
- She acts like she knows *everything*.
- Your parents will let her do all kinds of things that you aren't allowed to do.
- She gets all the new outfits and you have to wear hand-me-downs (even though her favorite color is green, which you hate).

I can think of a lot more reasons, but I would need more paper. Everyone is always surprised to find out Lucinda is my sister. This is because stuff has never spilled on her shirt and her hair never sticks up. She always remembers to say thank you, please, and excuse me. My sister always has her homework done on time, she never snorts when she laughs. Oh, and she can fly.

My sister is a pain.

I lay underneath the hedge in front of my school so I could peek out onto the sidewalk. There was large sign announcing COTTINGLEY FAIRY ACADEMY: TRAINING SPRITES IN THE ART OF FAIRY GODMOTHERING SINCE 1254. Of course the sign was enchanted, so when any humans looked over all they saw was the brass plaque that said COTTINGLEY PRIVATE SCHOOL in front of a small brick building. Our actual school was the size of a castle, but obviously that would stick out, so it was enchanted too.

A group of kids were coming. I hunkered down so they wouldn't see me. It was the same group that walked by every morning on the way to their school. I'd been studying them since the summer. As a fairy godmother to-be, I was focused on learning all about humans, or humdrums as we called them, even though I was still only sprite status 2. It was important if I was going to be able to grant wishes someday.

"Willow? What are you doing down there?" My sister wrinkled up her nose. "Your clothes are getting all dirty."

I spun around to glare at her. Why did my sister

have to be so nosy *and* so loud? I motioned for her to be quiet. The girl named Miranda was in the middle of all of her friends. I scribbled down in my notebook what she was wearing.

"Are you spying on them?" Lucinda asked loud enough so they turned around to look as they went by. I scooted out from under the hedge quickly and whacked against the school sign. I stood up, brushing off my shirt. There was a big grass stain on the sleeve.

"I told you you'd get dirty." Lucinda crossed her arms. She was only thirteen, but she acted like she was all grown up. "Why don't you read about Humdrums in books like everyone else?"

"I like them; they're interesting."

Another girl wandered by, singing out loud with her music player. She would take a couple steps, stop and do a shimmy dance, and then start walking again. Her outfit had every color in the rainbow. Lucinda looked at me with one eyebrow raised.

"Okay," I admit, "she's a weird one, but those other girls were interesting."

The girl saw us standing by the school gate. She took out her earphones and waved as she walked past. "Hi!"

Lucinda's mouth pressed into a thin line before

giving a stiff wave back. "Great, now the Humdrum is paying attention to us."

"This isn't my fault." I hoped I wouldn't get in trouble. Fairies weren't supposed to attract human attention.

"Just like the mud all over your uniform isn't your fault?"

Before I could say anything, my shirt puffed out with a whistle of wind and all the dirt and mud popped off and drifted back to the ground.

I spun around. "Grandma!" She was leaning against the school gate, her silver hair pulled back into a bun.

"We're not supposed to use magic to grant our own wishes," Lucinda said. "It's against the rules. Number 10.4.01A."

"Grandmas are allowed to break rules." Grandma gave me a wink. "Especially when our granddaughters have a big birthday coming up."

Lucinda's mouth pinched shut. She was not a fan of breaking the rules. I also didn't think she's a big fan of fun. I didn't have much when she was around, that's for sure.

"Are you coming to school today?" I asked. My grandma had a full time wish-granting job in the human world as the principal of the Humdrum school, but sometimes she would teach a class for us.

"I just stopped by to drop off some cupcakes." Grandma pulled a box tied with pink twine out from behind her back. In glittery letters it said across the top ENCHANTED SUGAR BAKERY.

I clapped my hands together. Enchanted Sugar was the best bakery in town, even the Humdrums thought so. My mom owned the bakery and made the best cupcakes in the whole world.

"Her birthday isn't until tomorrow," Lucinda pointed out.

"I think birthday cupcakes belong on Monday, it makes the week sweeter. Besides, I wanted to give you my present early." She pulled a thick silver envelope covered with polka dots from her pocket.

I peeled the flap of the envelope open and slid out a thick piece of white paper. In shiny gold writing it said:

THIS CERTIFICATE ENTITLES WILLOW THALIA DOYLE TO ATTEND RIVERSIDE ELEMENTARY SCHOOL (A HUMDRUM SCHOOL) FOR A PERIOD OF TWO WEEKS.

My mouth fell open. I threw my arms around Grandma. This was going to be the best birthday ever!

☆ 5 ☆

two

There were three things I wanted for my birthday:

1. To be an only child
2. To have a dog
3. To make a best friend of my very own

Even though I want to be an only child, there is no way my parents would get rid of my older sister. They seem to really like her. However, I was hoping the other two would come true. I know two things sounds like a lot, but it's my tenth birthday. That's a big deal. The big one-oh. Double digits. If there was a time to get what you really want, then this would be it.

I was supposed to be paying attention to our class on magical history, but I couldn't stop thinking about my grandma's present. I stuck my hand in my skirt pocket to touch the envelope to prove to myself it was real. I couldn't wait to get home and figure out what I would wear tomorrow.

"Willow?"

My head snapped up. Ms. Sullivan, our teacher, and the rest of my class were all staring at me.

"Yes, Ma'am?"

"I asked you to list the main causes of the Hiding."

I relaxed, at least it was an easy question. Hundreds of years ago Humdrums and fairies had been friends. Then some fairies decided it was more fun to play tricks on humans instead of granting wishes. The Humdrums didn't like that at all and tried to lock up all the fairies they could find. Fairies had to go into hiding until Humdrums forgot we existed at all. We used magic to blend in, to disappear right under their noses, just like our school. Now they thought we were just imaginary. The Department of Fairy Safety decided it was safer that way and it would be better to avoid getting too close. The whole thing was messed up if you asked me. How were we supposed to grant wishes for Humdrums if we didn't really know them?

"Ms. Sullivan, what do you think Humdrums would do if they knew we existed?" I asked, ignoring her question.

A boy in our class, Milo, grabbed his throat and fell into the aisle pretending to choke. He rolled back and forth, making faces. The two Van Elder twins started giggling. They were boy crazy. Even over Milo, who used to pick his nose up until last year. Ms. Sullivan rapped her desk with her wand and everyone went silent. No one messed with Ms. Sullivan when she had her wand out.

"Milo, you should try out for the Academy play if you want to practice your dramatics. As for your question, Willow, you don't need to worry about the Humdrums figuring out you're a fairy while you are on your Humdrum visit. I'm sure it will go just fine."

Trumpets blasted in the hallway, indicating school was over. Everyone stuffed their books in their cubby and started to grab their things.

"Don't forget to bring your permission slips back for the dragon farm!" Ms. Sullivan called out as everyone started to leave. "If you don't have a slip, you can't go on the field trip."

Sasha and Adele stopped at my desk. They were my best friends. They were great, but they were friends with each other first. This made them each other's *best* best friend and me the extra. The only other girls in my class were the Van Elder twins. They looked alike and were always finishing each other's sentences. And there was no way I was going to be best friends with Milo the former booger-eater.

This is one problem with being a fairy; there aren't enough of us to go around for everyone to have a best friend of their own. That's why I wanted to go to the Humdrum school. I didn't plan to tell anyone I was a fairy, but I did plan to make a friend. After all it was my birthday; if there was ever a time to get something I wished for, this would be it.

three

How you know it's going to be a bad day:
a. You're in trouble before you've even had a chance to brush your teeth.
b. You almost killed your know-it-all-sort-of-had-it-coming sister in a tragic magazine accident.
c. You're going to be late for your first day at Humdrum school.
d. Your pet hamster, Lester, is suddenly purple and the size of a pony. Hamsters should never weigh over two hundred pounds.
e. All of the above.

Today was turning into an *e*, all of the above, kind of day.

Lester slammed into the bookcase. Then he whirled around and ran in the opposite direction. He didn't seem happy about his new size. It was understandable. Lester was used to being a normal hamster.

"Take it easy." I made my voice calm. Lucinda was standing on top of the sofa with her hands over her eyes.

I thought it was unfair that she wasn't helping since she was the one who turned Lester into a giant purple pony-sized hamster. It was extra unfair because Lucinda's always talking how since she's older, she's so much better at everything. Now we had a real emergency on our hands and she was no help at all. It was too early in the morning for this.

"Everything's okay." I was wearing my dad's skiing goggles, Lucinda's soccer knee pads, and some oven mitts. Lester's generally a pretty good hamster, but sometimes he bites.

Lester tried to scurry under the dining room table, but he barely fit. His shaking made the table rock back and forth.

"What's going on down here?" My mom shuffled into the room and put her hands on her hips. She didn't panic when she saw a giant hamster in her dining room.

When you have a fairy godmother for a mom it takes more than a bit of magic gone wrong to rattle her.

Mom sighed like she was really tired, even though she just got up. "Okay, someone needs to start explaining."

"Lucinda did it," I said.

Her eyes narrowed. "Willow hit me with a magazine."

"I didn't know it was her. And she was in my room. *And* she's the one who did this to Lester. He's academy property." I pointed out the last bit because my mom was really big on being extra careful with stuff that didn't belong to you.

Lester lumbered out from under the table and made a run for the kitchen. He didn't make it three steps before my mom waved her finger in his direction.

There was a *POP* and then Lester was back to being hamster sized. I hurried over and picked him up, dropping him into his box. He scurried into one of his favorite toilet paper tubes. Mom surveyed the mess in the room. She snapped her fingers and the broom and bucket raced out of the kitchen and began cleaning up.

Lucinda sat on the sofa with Mom looking closely at her face. "It feels like my nose is broken. I can't go to school with a broken nose," she wailed.

"Willow, what were you thinking?" Mom asked,

shaking her head. "You could have really hurt your sister."

"I didn't do it on purpose," I pointed out. I didn't feel that bad about smacking my sister with a rolled-up magazine. In a Humdrum family it wouldn't be a big deal to hit your sister with a magazine, but there was nothing normal about our family. When I hit my sister she'd been the size of a horsefly. If Lucinda hadn't dodged to the left at the last minute, she would have been a sparkly smear on the wall.

"I thought she was a bug," I tried to explain.

"I don't look anything like a bug, I look like Tinkerbell," Lucinda snarled. She hated when I called her a bug. She *did* look like a bug when she was flying, even if she didn't want to admit it.

"What were you doing in my room anyway?"

"I was practicing my flying." Lucinda raised her chin in the air. My sister never missed a single chance to mention that she could fly. If you said there was a tornado coming, she would point out how hard it is to fly in high winds.

"Enough of that. Now, what happened to Lester?" Mom asked.

I crossed my arms. I wanted to hear how Lucinda was going to explain this.

"I don't know. When she hit me I must have made a spell. I don't remember. She hit me really hard." Lucinda rubbed her temple.

I sucked in a deep breath. She was lying! "You looked right at him and did it. You did it on purpose."

"I couldn't do it on purpose. Sprites at my level aren't allowed to do animal magic unsupervised," Lucinda said.

I wished I could whack her again with another magazine. This time I wouldn't miss. I took a deep breath. I wasn't going to let her ruin both my birthday and my first day at Humdrum school. Everyone knew I was interested in humans, but what they didn't know is that what I really wanted was to be one. If I couldn't be a Humdrum, then I wanted the next best thing: to be best friends with one. I even knew which one. I'd been watching the girl named Miranda since the summer. She was blond and pretty. She always had a million friends around her and had a nice laugh. Miranda looked like the Humdrums that were on TV or in catalogs. She was perfect, and if everything went well, she was going to be my new best friend by the end of the day.

four

Why you might want a Humdrum for a friend:

a. A Humdrum friend is never going to turn your hamster purple or brag about how they can fly and you can't.

b. Because all the fairies in your school already have a best friend, which means you're left being the second-level friend, which is never as good.

c. Both A and B.

I rushed downstairs and grabbed my lunch bag off the counter.

"Whoa there. You go much faster and you're going to be flying," my dad said. He was sitting at the kitchen table reading the *Fairy Daily* newspaper.

"I doubt she'll fly. My teacher says it's rare these days

to have two flyers in the same family," Lucinda said, chewing her cereal.

"I wouldn't want to fly anyway." Sure, flying looked cool, but it wasn't much use. Unless your feet were sore and you didn't want to walk, it didn't seem like that great of a talent to have. I grabbed Lester in his hamster ball. "I'm going to be late."

"You're taking the mouse to school?"

"He's a hamster. I'm taking him for my first day to show them something from the Academy." I'd read that Humdrum kids liked animals. "Grandma took his cage to school already and she'll take him back to Cottingley after school."

"He makes your room smell funny," Lucinda said.

"You smell funny," I said. I could tell Lucinda was going to say something nasty, but my mom stopped her by putting her hand on Lucinda's shoulder.

"Before you run off, we have a present for you." Mom pulled a box covered in sparkling purple paper out from under the table.

I yanked off the paper. I knew what I asked for was special, which was only fair because I was turning ten. People don't turn double digits every day. It was a big deal birthday. The kind of birthday when

I might get what I really, really, *really* wanted: a dog.

My parents told me we couldn't get a dog, but I'm hoping they were just saying that to throw me off the track. Parents do that kind of thing all the time. The box could have water bowls and a leash in it. Anything's possible when it's your birthday.

I held my breath when I opened the box. Inside the tissue paper was a stuffed dog. I lifted it out looking for a note that might say that there was a real dog waiting in the yard. Nothing.

"A stuffed animal?" Lucinda's nose wrinkled up. She didn't say it, but you could tell what she was thinking: baby toy.

It was cute, but it wasn't the same as a real dog with a wagging tail and everything.

"It's the next best thing to a puppy," Mom said. "We can't have a dog around the house. It's just too risky." The stuffed dog made a tin-sounding robotic bark. "Your dad enchanted it so it barks."

"I suppose that's better than a real dog. Real dogs shed all over everything," Lucinda said even though no one asked her anything.

"You can get dogs that don't shed," I pointed out.

"A dog could eat me by accident when I was flying."

I tried to keep the smile off my face as I pictured a fluffy white puppy jumping up and swallowing my sister in one big gulp. I've wanted a dog as long as I can remember. But I didn't want one just because it might eat my sister. If that ever happened, it would just be a bonus. I put the box down on the table.

"Are you sure about this school visit?" Mom asked. "What if your magic power shows up today with all those Humdrums around?"

"She'll be fine." Dad smiled. "I did a two-week visit to a Humdrum school when I was her age. It's a great way to study them. Fascinating creatures."

"I'd rather read about them," Lucinda said.

"I think it will be neat to meet some, maybe even make a friend," I said.

Lucinda dropped her spoon in her cereal. "Humdrums and fairies aren't friends. It's against the rules. What if they figure out we're magical?"

"Calm down, Lucinda. Your sister didn't mean that she wanted to be friends with a Humdrum, just that she would be friendly with them." My mom smiled at me. I didn't say anything because that way I wouldn't have to lie. I really *did* want to be friends with a Humdrum.

"Now, if anything goes wrong or if your power shows up and you need help, you find your grandma right away," my dad said. "We can come pick you up and cut the whole visit short."

"But Grandma made it so I could visit for two whole weeks."

"You can't be in Humdrum school when you've got your power. You'll need to learn how to use it," Lucinda said.

"Just because it's my birthday doesn't mean I'll get my power. Lots of people don't get their magic on their birthday anymore," I pointed out. I hoped mine wouldn't show up for a long time. Like maybe never.

"Mine showed up first thing. I floated right out of bed," Lucinda said.

"You're my gold-star girl," Dad said. Lucinda sat up straighter and smiled. I rolled my eyes, grabbed my lunch bag, and left.

You would think being a part of a fairy godmother family would be fun, but it's not. You can't use magic whenever you want. You have to go to sprite training. You don't even get your magical abilities until you turn ten (if then). No one even believes in fairy godmothers anymore, so you're stuck granting wishes in secret. You can't be friends with Humdrums. And you can't have a dog because it might eat your stupid sister.

Life's really unfair sometimes.

five

Benefits of being a Humdrum (versus being a fairy):

- Your hamster is never the size of a pony.
- You get to make wishes instead of worrying about granting them for other people.
- You might have to clean your room as a Humdrum, but you never have to spend a whole Saturday collecting pixie dust for your mom. (The stuff makes me sneeze.)
- There are lots of Humdrums, which means there are lots of potential best friends to choose from.

I stood outside on the sidewalk in front of the Humdrum school, Riverside Elementary. Humdrum kids ran past me up the walk and over to the paved playground on the side of the building. I smoothed down my shirt and tried to relax. It felt like I had butterflies in my stomach. More than anything, even more than I wanted a dog, I wanted a best friend. I was hoping I might see Miranda outside and she would ask me my name and then we would start talking and before you knew it we'd be friends. So far I hadn't seen her.

As soon as I saw the gift from my grandma, I knew this was my chance. I'd spent the whole summer studying the Humdrums. It started because I told a small lie to my parents about how the magic mirror in the bathroom got a chip (never stand in front of a mirror practicing your dance moves and singing into your hairbrush, because you might accidently hit it and the stupid mirror will tell on you). As punishment they made me watch Humdrum TV. It was the best punishment EVER! Humdrums were really interesting. I watched the most popular TV shows and went to the Humdrum library and looked at their magazines. Even after my punishment was over I'd get my mom to take me to the mall. I watched them in the food court and listened in on their conversations. It was at the mall I'd seen Miranda for the first time. She was clearly a very popular Humdrum. Other girls copied what she wore and how she cut her hair. She was pretty and had a nice laugh. I could already imagine how great it would be to be her best friend.

I had watched those Humdrum shows carefully. I had the right clothes to fit in. I even had a list of things to talk about with my classmates folded up in the pocket of my backpack in case I needed to jump-start the conversation. Despite what my sister said, I knew Humdrums and fairies could be best friends.

Maybe it wouldn't be a good idea to have them come over to our house, though. My family might be well respected in the fairy community, but we were awfully strange compared to the Humdrums. Mom still dressed like it was the 1950s, with giant poodle skirts that flared out from her waist, and Dad, instead of having a normal lawn like everyone else, made these huge animals out of our bushes. Right now we had a dragon that snaked across the front of the house with bright red geranium flowers shooting out of its mouth like fire. Our Humdrum neighbors didn't stop by very often. But sometimes you would see them in their yards staring over at us.

I tucked the hamster ball under my arm and headed toward the school gate. There was no point in waiting for Miranda anymore; I'd have to wait until later to meet her.

"You're such a weirdo," a voice said.

I spun around and saw a girl with black curly hair that seemed to explode out of her head walking up to me. She was also dressed like no Humdrum I've ever seen. She had a white T-shirt, a flouncy ballerina-like tutu skirt, and regular lace-up brown shoes.

"Hey, I'm Katie." She stuck one hand out. I didn't shake it. It looked to me like she chewed her fingernails.

"Why did you call me weird?" I tried not to sound annoyed. I'd picked out my outfit very carefully. There was nothing strange about me. I looked her up and down. I didn't want to be mean, but it didn't seem like she should be calling anyone weird.

"I didn't say anything. You must be the new girl. I heard you were going to visit our class for a couple weeks. Don't you like your old school?" she asked. "I saw you there the other day at the gate. I waved hi."

"Someone called me weird."

"Wow, you're really stressed. Does the idea of a new school freak you out? The first day of school used to upset my best friend. She would throw up. She moved away this summer. What's your name?"

"Willow."

"I never heard of anyone named that before."

"It's a family name."

"Don't worry, I like names that are different."

Katie started walking toward the door. She paused, waiting for me to walk with her.

"Do you like to dance? I want to be a ballerina when I grow up, or a soccer player. I also think it would be cool to be an astronaut."

I found it hard to keep up with Katie's conversation. "I'm not really sure what I'll be."

Just then Miranda and her friends brushed past us on their way inside. I took a step forward, but she was already walking past. I missed my chance!

"Hey, is that a hamster?" Katie must have noticed for the first time I was carrying Lester.

"He's the class pet from my school. I brought him today because I thought people might like to see something from the Academy."

"I have a parrot. Her name is Crackers."

I couldn't tell if she was telling the truth. Maybe it was an imaginary parrot. The bell rang as we walked up the stairs to the school.

"I have to go sign in with the office."

"Okay, I'll see you later," Katie yelled out, doing a twirl on her toes. She stumbled and bounced off one of the lockers. First Humdrum I meet in my new school and she's stranger than any of the fairies in my old school.

"Weirdo."

I whirled around, but Katie was gone. I looked up and down the hall. How dare she call me weird again? I decided that if I saw Katie again, I would ignore her. I had enough crazy in my life.

six

Reasons grandmas can be really cool:
  a. They almost always have candy at their house.
  b. They tell great stories about when your parents were little.
  c. They aren't as fussy about the rules (sometimes they even let you jump on the bed, which even a stuck-up thirteen-year-old likes to do sometimes).
  d. When they ask you a question, they really listen to your answer.

My shoes squeaked on the tile floor as I walked down to the office. My grandma's name, Ms. Glinda Doyle, was in raised silver letters on her office door. I tapped and it swung open.

Grandma's office didn't look like what you would

expect in a Humdrum principal's office. She had a rug on the floor, red and gold with tassels. Her desk was a dark wood with carved legs. The walls were painted the color of hot chocolate and decorated with bright pictures. When she saw it was me she leaped out of her office chair.

"Happy birthday, Willow." She bent over and gave me a huge hug.

"Thanks." The carpet lurched under my feet.

"Careful, it's a magic carpet." Grandma stomped on the floor and it stopped moving. "Got the darn thing when I traveled through Istanbul. I should have known it was on sale for a reason."

"Does it really fly?"

"Oh, it flies—not well, but it flies. I thought the desk would be enough to hold it down, but sometimes it gets uppity." She stomped on it one more time. The tassels fluttered and then lay down.

"Thanks for arranging this visit for me. It's the best gift ever."

"I have you signed up for Mrs. Caul's class. You'll like her. If anyone asks, tell them you're visiting for two weeks to see if you want to transfer schools."

"I'm ready. I studied Humdrums all last summer. I

know what they like to wear and their favorite music and games. "

"I knew this was the perfect gift for you." Grandma smiled. "And who knows what could happen?"

I nodded. "I'll do my best to fit in."

"Keep in mind, there isn't just one sort of Humdrum. They come in all shapes and sizes, all sorts of likes and dislikes—just like fairies."

I knew Grandma was right, but I could tell that while there might be all kinds of Humdrums, there were clearly some who were better than others. I didn't want just anyone to be my friend, I wanted someone special. After all, she was going to be my very *best* friend. "Grandma, do you think it will ever be possible for Humdrums and fairies to be friends?"

"That's a hard question." Grandma rubbed her chin while she thought about it. "They're afraid to believe in magic and we're afraid of what they would do if they knew we were real. So we each stick to our own sides and now nobody knows how to meet in the middle anymore."

"Seems silly to do something just because of something that happened hundreds of years ago."

"Sure does. A lot of things grown-ups do are silly,

but you never know when things might change; all it takes is one person." A bell rang in the hallway. "I better walk you down to your class. We don't want you to be late on your first day."

The hallway was bustling with kids rushing to class. Everyone had time to smile when they saw my grandma.

"Hey! I just found my iPod. I thought I lost it," a girl said, pulling the music player out of her bag.

"Guess what!" a boy called out to his friend. "My parents decided I could sign up for flag football after all." They high-fived each other.

I glanced over at my grandma. This was an awfully lucky hallway. "Are you granting wishes?"

She winked. "Best part of working here. Kids have great wishes."

I chewed on my lip. I knew grandma was a Fairy Godmother Level 3, which should have meant she could work anywhere. Working in schools was considered a Level 1 job. "Do you like working here?"

"I love it." She stopped walking and looked me right in the face. "People might think that grown-up wishes are more important. I think kid wishes are pretty important too. Maybe more important than adult wishes. Kids still believe in magic. They know small things are sometimes what really matter." She stopped walking. "Well, here we are. I put a small cage in the room this morning for your hamster. I'll take him back to Cottingley tonight after school." Grandma licked her thumb and wiped a smudge off my cheek. "You ready?"

I looked in the doorway. The classroom was full of kids standing in groups, laughing and talking. I could see the teacher standing at the front. She was smiling. I closed my eyes and made my wish for a best friend again.

I still believe in magic too.

seven

Kinds of kids in my class:
- Kids who are really good at art
- Kids who are really good at sports
- Kids with fancy clothes
- Kids who are shy

Kinds of kids who want to hang out with me:
- Nobody

Recess wasn't over, but I had come in early. I pulled up a chair next to Lester's cage. He was sound asleep in a pile of cedar shavings. His breath poofed out his cheeks and blew the shavings near his mouth away. Then he would suck them back close with the next breath. I tapped on the side of the glass. Lester opened one eye and looked at me. It was hard to tell with a hamster, but he looked annoyed. I sighed. I shouldn't have woken him up. I just wanted to see a friendly face.

The day wasn't turning out the way I had hoped. I was wearing all the right clothes. I knew all the right stuff about every popular band and TV show out there, but I still didn't fit in. It was like they knew I was different. Plus everyone already had a best friend. Miranda had two, Bethany and Paula. I was going to have to get in line to be her friend and she didn't look like she wanted anymore. The only one who talked to me was the weird girl, Katie.

The bell rang and everyone ran back inside, laughing and joking.

"Hey, I couldn't find you," Katie said.

"I had to come inside and take care of Lester. He gets lonely." We both looked down at Lester. He was making tiny hamster snores. "He's really tired."

"I guess so." Katie sounded unsure.

"All right, everybody settle down. We're going to work on making a poster for the hallway to represent our class," Mrs. Caul said. She clapped her hands to get everyone's attention.

"Willow, can you help me by getting out all the

poster paints?" Mrs. Caul asked, pointing at the cabinet. I jumped to attention and bent under the class sink to get the giant squeeze bottles. I pulled a bunch out onto the counter.

"Is there orange?" Miranda asked. "I want to use orange."

I felt my face flush. Miranda was talking to me. She'd even started the conversation! My mind raced to think of the advice from the magazines I'd been reading all summer. There were all sorts of articles on making friends.

"Orange is my favorite color too," I said. Maybe Miranda would see that we had lots in common.

"It isn't my favorite color. I just need it for what I want to make," Miranda said. She looked annoyed.

"Me too; I mean I like it a lot, it's one of my favorites, but not my *favorite* favorite."

Miranda stood looking at me. I plastered a smile on my face. Maybe it would cover up the fact I couldn't think of anything to say. I could pull out my list of topics, but I was sure that would be bad. None of the Humdrums seemed to need a list of things to talk about. Being normal was harder than it looked. I was finally having a conversation with the most popular girl in my class and I was blowing it. If I could only come up with something, anything, to say.

"Oh, for crying out loud, ask anything. Ask her why her hair looks so silly," a voice yelled in my ear. I was so surprised I jumped, squeezing the purple paint bottle that was in my hand. In slow motion I watched the stream of paint squirt out of the bottle and splash down on Miranda's fuzzy cream-colored sweater. Uh-oh.

"Look at what you did!" Miranda yelled. She wiped at the paint, smearing it.

I stared at the giant splotch of paint on her sweater. "I'm—I'm sorry," I stammered.

"Willow just splashed me with paint," Miranda yelled to Mrs. Caul. I could feel everyone staring at me.

"I didn't do it on purpose. I was surprised because . . . ," I whirled around to see who had yelled. Katie was standing behind me. I pointed at her. "She scared me when she yelled in my ear. That's what made me spray the paint."

"I didn't yell anything," Katie said.

"You did too, you called Miranda's hair stupid."

"Hey!" Miranda protested. "My hair looks fine. My mom did it."

Miranda looked really mad. Her one hand kept

patting her hair to make sure it was still in place. She still had a giant purple paint polka dot on her sweater.

"I think your hair looks great. It wasn't me, it was her." I pointed again at Katie. If I was going to be honest, I did think Miranda's hair was a bit too poofy, but never would have said a thing to her about it.

Mrs. Caul took me by the elbow. "Willow, I was standing near Katie. She didn't say anything. No one yelled anything." Her voice was calm and soft.

"But she did," I said. I looked around to see if anyone else would agree with me. No one met my eyes. I felt like I was going to start crying. Great. Now I would be known as the new girl who has no friends, is a crybaby, and hears voices.

"It's okay, it was an accident. Accidents happen. I'm sure Miranda knows you didn't mean it," Mrs. Caul said.

Miranda didn't look like she knew any such thing. Her arms were crossed and her face was all scrunched up. I wasn't crazy; Katie *had* yelled right in my ear.

"Miranda, take the hall pass and go down to the washroom and rinse off your sweater. You can put on one of the paint smocks until your shirt dries." Mrs. Caul clapped her hands again, encouraging everyone to get back to their projects.

"It better come out." Miranda stomped past me to the bathroom.

I stood by the window, trying to keep from crying. The only sound was the squeak of Lester running on his exercise wheel.

eight

Things that would make today a better day:
- If I found out it was a dream and I could start all over
- If my sister decided to move far away
- If it never happened at all

As soon as the bell rang, I bolted out of school. I didn't even try to find my grandma. The last thing I wanted to do was go to Cottingley with her to take Lester back. Everyone would ask me how my first day went. It was bad enough living it, I didn't want to talk about it too. I walked home, kicking leaves and mumbling to myself. I'd gone to Humdrum school only one day and everything was ruined. Not only did I not make any friends, but I was pretty sure Miranda hated me. And no matter what everyone else said, I *had* heard someone yell in my ear. It was one thing to study Humdrums, but they were a lot harder to deal with in person.

HOOOOOOONK!!

I whipped around. A small black dog was in the middle of the road, frozen in place while a car zoomed toward it. The car slammed on its brakes and started to skid. I squeezed my eyes shut. I didn't want to see what would happen. The tires screeched and I waited for the nasty icky thud sound that would prove, once and for all, that this was the worst day ever.

"Stupid dog!" the man in the car yelled. I opened my eyes to see the car peel out.

The dog ran to the side of the road. He stood there shaking. I bent down to make sure he was okay. He was a Scottie dog with bushy eyebrows who needed a bath and a good brushing. I let him sniff my hand and then gave him a pat.

"You're okay. That guy was a jerk. And he was speeding." I rubbed his ears, which he seemed to like. The dog wasn't wearing a collar. "Are you lost?"

The dog looked at me, his tail thumping on the ground. He leaned forward and licked the end of my nose. Then he rested his muzzle on my shoulder. It was the nicest thing that had happened all day. I started crying. I know you should be careful with stray dogs, but I couldn't help myself. I hugged him. I didn't even mind that he smelled a bit like garbage. I buried my face in his fuzz.

"Careful, water curls my fur."

My throat froze shut. I sat straight up and looked at the dog. He stared right back.

"Who said that?" I called out, looking around.

"You don't need to yell; I'm sitting right here."

I yanked the dog closer. I bet my sister and her friends were doing some sort of magic spell. "You're talking. That's impossible."

"And you're listening. Trust me, that's the surprising part. I talk all the time, but humans don't ever notice." The dog gave a shake to put his fur back in place. "You try to say something important and all they say back is 'nice doggie.' It can be really annoying. My name's Winston." He offered a paw.

"You're talking," I said again.

The dog cocked his head to the side. "You okay? You're repeating yourself."

"Dogs don't talk."

"Of course we do. How else would we communicate?

If you want a tricky question, ask yourself how it's possible you can hear me. Humans never do."

"I'm not human. I'm fairy."

"Fairy, as in godmother? Really? I've heard about your type, but I've never met one." Winston gave my leg a sniff to check things out.

"I'm not a fairy godmother yet. I'm still at sprite level. I can't even . . ." My voice trailed off as things fell into place. My mouth fell open in surprise and I touched my ear softly.

"Can't even what?"

I wiggled my fingers to see if I felt any different. I'd obviously gotten my special power. I could talk to animals. I'd heard that some fairies could do it, but I'd never met any. My heart was beating faster. "I can do magic," I said softly. "I can talk to animals."

"Able to do magic. Fascinating. The most impressive thing I can do is dig a giant hole. I'm also quite good at shoe chewing. I can take a heel completely off a shoe in under five minutes."

I wasn't paying too much attention to what he was saying. I kept thinking about what happened at school. The pieces fell into place. "Do you know what this means? If I can talk to animals, then I wasn't hearing things today. I must have heard Lester!" Lester was the one to say Miranda's hair was silly. And he called me weird too. That wasn't very nice, considering all the carrots I'd given him.

"Lester?"

"Lester is our school hamster," I explained. "He said some things, but I thought someone else said it and it sort of got me into trouble." I felt bad about blaming Katie.

"Shouldn't listen to rats." Winston nodded wisely. "Much better sticking to dogs if you ask me. If this power of yours is new, you're going to have to think about whom you listen to. Cats could be trouble too. Shifty."

"Lester isn't a rat," I said. "Besides it wasn't really his fault. I didn't realize he was talking to me. He never did before, or if he did then I didn't hear him."

I suppose I should have been happy. My special power had shown up and it was pretty cool. Way better than flying, in my opinion. Talking to animals was useful. Flying was just flashy. Now I could start the next level of sprite training. My parents would be excited, but I felt sad. Once my parents knew I had my power, they would want me to go straight back to the

Academy. I wasn't going to have a chance to get to know any Humdrums; I'd be too busy learning to wish-grant. I stood up and brushed off my pants; might as well go home and tell everyone the news. Winston fell in step with me as I walked home.

"Whatever trouble you're in, I'm sure it can't be that bad," Winston said.

"It's not that. Part of me hoped I wouldn't get a power at all, or at least not right away."

"Why not?"

"If I didn't get my power, then I wouldn't have to be a fairy godmother."

"Why is that a bad thing?"

"I don't want to spend my time learning how to grant Humdrum—human—wishes. I want to *be* a Humdrum. It's not like I'll ever be as good a fairy as my sister is, so why bother? I always wanted to do a Humdrum school visit and now after one day they'll make me stop. They'll tell me I can do it some other time, but that's just a grown-up's way of saying no." I kicked a pile of leaves on the sidewalk. One of them fluttered down and stuck to the side of Winston's beard. "I'll never have a best friend. And I met the perfect person to be my friend too. Her name is Miranda."

"I'm sure you can do whatever you set your mind to."

"But, because I have my power, my parents are going to expect me to go back to the Fairy Academy."

"Then don't tell them you got your power," Winston said. "No one can tell you can talk to animals unless you tell them. Keep going to school until you make best friends with this Miranda person. If it was up to me, I would pick someone who owned a restaurant or deli to be my best friend."

Winston kept walking, no doubt thinking about shaved bologna or chicken with gravy, but I stopped. My mind was spinning faster than Lester's hamster wheel. I had never told a lie to my parents. Okay, I'd never told them a *big*, important lie. They would be really mad if they found out.

On the other hand, I didn't have to tell the truth right away. After all, getting your magical power was a pretty big deal. My dad was always saying how people needed to think before they acted. I could take some time to get used to the new me before I told everyone. While I did that, I could keep going to Riverside Elementary. Maybe get invited to a slumber party or something. You could say what I was doing was like a science experiment for school. It wasn't a lie exactly, it was just telling the truth late.

"Winston, you're a genius," I said.

"Yes, I know," Winston said.

"How can I thank you?"

Winston stopped and looked serious. "Do you mean it?" he asked, wagging his tail slightly. "The thing is, I'm between homes. I could use a place to stay."

My smile disappeared. "I wish you could stay with me, but my parents would never let me. Trust me, I've been asking for a dog for years. They're afraid a dog would eat my sister, Lucinda."

"Is she tasty?" Winston's eyebrows drew together in confusion.

"I wouldn't think so." I thought about it. "I think she would taste like boiled cauliflower, but I don't know for sure."

"What if I promised to not eat her? As long as there was other food around I'm pretty sure I could resist the temptation."

"My parents wouldn't want to take a chance," I said.

Winston nodded sadly, his tail dropped. "I understand. I suppose I should get going," Winston said. "Good luck with the magic thing."

I bent down and rubbed Winston's ears one more time. Winston gave my hand a quick lick and then headed off through someone's front lawn. If I told my parents that Winston promised not to eat Lucinda, I would also have to tell them I could understand him. That would mean the end of school and the best-friend plan. On the other hand, Winston was an awfully small dog to be out on his own.

"Winston! Wait a minute." It didn't seem right to let Winston leave. He wasn't a careful dog. He had already walked out in front of a car. "Do you want something to eat? We don't have any kibble, but we have cheese at the house."

"Cheese?" Winston's nose twitched. "I happen to have a fondness for cheese." Winston scampered back across the lawn and sat next to me. His tail was whipping back and forth.

"Then we're in luck. Come with me." It was good to see Winston looking so happy. If it hadn't been for him, I never would have had the idea—and I might not have discovered I had my power, either. Now all I had to do was figure out how to keep two secrets from my parents: a dog in the house, and the fact I could talk to the dog.

nine

Why dogs make the best pets ever:

1. They are fuzzy. It's much more fun to cuddle something fuzzy. If you try to cuddle a fish, it isn't going to turn out well.

2. Dogs love you all the time. Even when you're cranky or if you spill stuff on your clothes.

3. Unlike stuffed animals, real dogs will lick you when *you* need attention. They'll also chase a ball. Stuffed animals just sit there.

On the upside, stuffed animals never poop in the house.

I pushed the garage door open and peered inside. "Winston?"

I heard a rustle and then a muffled bump.

"Dang it."

"Winston? You okay?"

Winston padded out from behind a pile of recycling. There was a cobweb stuck to his eyebrows.

"Just how much stuff can one family fit into a garage?" Winston asked. "Did you know there is a giant circus tent back there?"

"Yeah. It's sort of a long story. Our garage is sort of bigger on the inside than it looks on the outside, it's a magic thing."

"And there's a golden carriage too."

"That's an even longer story." I felt a bit embarrassed. "Granting wishes sometimes requires supplies. My dad is big on having stuff handy just in case."

"No shame in being prepared."

"I can sneak you into the house now, but you have to be quiet."

Winston hunched down; his tail swished back and forth. "No worries. I'll be like a ninja. Quiet and deadly."

His tail hit a stack of tin cans for the recycling and they clattered to the floor. Each can let out a loud *CLANG* as it hit the cement floor. They bounced up and down like popcorn. Winston rushed over to try and stop them from rolling around, but he bumped into the side of my bike. The bike fell over and landed on the lawn mower with a screech of metal.

I winced. Being sneaky is supposed to be a quiet thing. I looked over my shoulder to see if anyone would come out to investigate. "Maybe it would be better if you didn't try to be a like a ninja from now on," I suggested.

We crept upstairs and slipped into the bathroom. I'd wanted a dog for a long time, but I preferred one not quite so stinky. He needed a bath.

Winston sat in the center of the tub surrounded by a sea of bubbles. "More bubbles, please." His tail wagged under the water, making waves.

"Are you sure?" I had already poured a half bottle of my sister's fancy bath gel into the tub.

"There is no such thing as too many bubbles." Winston put his muzzle in the bath water and snorted. A spray of water flew up.

"Willow!" Lucinda pounded on the door. "You've been in there forever."

"Go away! I'm in the bath." I looked around desperately. There was no place to hide Winston.

"I need to use the mirror." She pounded on the door again.

"Well, you can't. You have to wait."

"Don't be a baby, it will take me two seconds." Lucinda started to open the door.

Panicked, I jumped into the tub with all of my clothes on. I pushed a wave of bubbles over Winston so that he was completely covered. "Stay still," I hissed.

Lucinda came in and glanced at the water and bubbles that had sloshed over the side of the tub. "You are such a spaz." She stood in front of the mirror. "Mirror, mirror on the wall, how would I look with curly hair?" Miranda asked. Her image in the mirror blurred for a second and then she was looking back, her long blond hair curled into perfect ringlets. Lucinda turned her head to the side and studied how she looked.

"I can't believe you busted in so you could play with your hair."

"If you spent any time on your hair, it could look nice too, instead of looking like you cut it with the lawn mower." Lucinda looked over at me and then leaned in closer. "Are you wearing a shirt?"

I yanked my arm back under the water. "None of your business."

"MOM! Willow is wearing all her clothes in the bathtub!" Lucinda yelled down the stairs.

I clunked my head on the tile. I could see Winston's brown eyes blinking through a pile of soapsuds. I motioned at him and he hunkered farther down.

Mom peeked in the bathroom. "Okay, what's going on?"

"I'm trying to take a bath. It would be nice if I could do it without an audience." I glowered at my sister.

"She's wearing all her clothes." Lucinda crossed her arms. "In the tub. Who does that? It's crazy."

"Don't call your sister crazy." My mom rubbed her forehead. "Willow, is there a reason you're fully dressed in the tub?"

"I thought I would wash my clothes at the same time I washed myself. It saves water. It's earth-friendly." It wasn't a great reason, but it was the best I could come up with.

"Well, that's a nice idea," Mom said.

"Is there a problem?" Dad poked his head in the bathroom. I slouched down lower in the tub. Pretty soon we were going to have to invite the neighbors over. It was impossible to have any privacy in this house.

"Willow's taking a bath in her clothes to save water," my mom explained.

"Whatever," Lucinda butted in. "She should worry

less about the planet and more about why her magic didn't show up. Everyone else in this family got their powers on their birthday."

"Lucinda, why don't you go to your room and let your dad and me talk to your sister for a minute?" Mom waited until Lucinda left and then sat down on the edge of the tub.

My dad stood in the doorway. "I think it's nice you're taking an interest in the environment."

Mom looked over at him and he stopped talking. "Honey, is everything okay?"

"Everything's fine, Mom." Winston's small black nose poked through the suds. It wriggled back and forth for a moment. Uh-oh. It looked like he had to sneeze. I used my foot to push his head back under the bubbles.

"You know, there are lots of fairies who don't come into their magic until later," my mom said, patting my hand. "Things have changed; not everyone gets their powers on their birthday the way they used to. It doesn't mean anything's wrong."

"Lucinda's right, though; everyone in our family did get it on their birthday." Dad noticed Mom glaring at him. "Uh, not that it matters one way or the other. In fact, heck, maybe it's better to wait awhile."

"What if I didn't get my power at all?" I asked.

"You'd be like a Humdrum," my dad said. His mouth was wrinkled up.

"Would it be that bad if I was Humdrum?"

"Of course not. Your dad and I love you a hundred percent. But you don't need to worry. There's no reason to believe you won't get your magic."

"Okay." I watched the mound of bubbles near my knees to see if Winston's nose would poke up again.

"I tell you what, if your power hasn't shown up by Saturday then we'll go to Doctor Bumbershoot and have her look things over," my dad said. "We can make sure everything checks out."

"I don't want—" I started to say, but then Winston's nose stuck back out. "Okay. I'll go." His nose started to wiggle back and forth faster and faster. "Can I be alone now?"

Mom and Dad looked at each other. I was afraid they were going to just keep talking, but they left. The instant the door to the bathroom shut, Winston's head shot out of the water and he let out a huge sneeze. Bubbles flew into my face.

"Woo. Sorry about that. Turns out those soap

bubbles tickle." Winston shook, sending a spray of water around.

I wiped my face and stood up in the tub. My clothes were soaking wet. I yanked a towel off the rack and started to dry off.

"I can't believe my sister. If she didn't have to barge in here, then everything would have been fine. Now I'm stuck going to Bumbershoot's on Saturday."

"What's a Bumbershoot?"

"It's a who, not a what. She's sort of a fairy doctor. I hate going. Her cures are usually worse than whatever is wrong with you."

I lifted Winston out of the tub and draped a towel over him so he could shake off. The mirror rippled.

"Keep your mouth shut about the dog or you could find yourself falling off the wall," I warned the mirror. Keeping secrets in this house was almost impossible.

"If you really don't want to go to this Bumbershoot doctor, you could tell them your fairy power showed up," Winston said.

"No way, at least not yet. I've got two weeks at Humdrum school. If I leave after one day, I'll never have a chance to get to know Miranda. " My socks were making a squishy sound on the tile floor. "Who knows, if I try really hard maybe Miranda and I can be best friends by the end of this week and then I won't have to go Bumbershoot's."

ten

Making a best friend is harder than:
  a. putting together a million-piece jigsaw puzzle.
  b. swimming across the Pacific Ocean while wearing a cement bathing suit.
  c. climbing Mount Everest during the winter, through the snow, on your knees.
  d. just about anything you can imagine.

I had all sorts of ideas on how to make Miranda my best friend. I'd been hoping to make a best friend since I started studying Humdrums so I was sure one of my plans would work. I kept notes in my diary at home of how the rest of the week went.

TUESDAY

Plan: Bring peanut butter cookies from my mom's bakery to give to Miranda.

Result: Turns out Miranda has a peanut allergy. Her best friend Bethany smacked them out of my hand and accused me of trying to kill her. Then Katie picked them off the ground, brushed them off, and ate them. She said cookies should never be wasted.

WEDNESDAY

Plan: Found a cool pencil that had a giant pink flamingo on the top (with feathers!) that I know Miranda would like. Will stick the pencil in Miranda's desk when everyone else is out on recess. Once she says how much she likes it, I will admit I gave it to her.

Result: Just before I could tell Miranda the pencil was from me, Stewart, who sits in the back of the class and sometimes eats his own boogers, said he gave it to her. Miranda made a face and dropped the pencil.

At the end of the day it was still on the floor. Thought Katie might pick it up, but it appears she doesn't like pink stuff. Or she is also grossed out by the idea of Stewart boogers.

THURSDAY

Plan: Lean against the wall near Miranda so she can notice that I am wearing a T-shirt that has the logo for her favorite band on it. Once she sees that we have the same taste in music, she will invite me over to her house and share her playlist with me.

Result: Miranda, Bethany, and Adele started laughing. Couldn't figure out why. Katie was the only one to tell me that the artwork on the wall was still wet and I had paint all over the back of my shirt.

FRIDAY

Plan: Use my new magic to have three butterflies land on Miranda's head. Butterflies are her favorite thing (based on all the butterfly stickers she puts on everything). I will point them out to her, hold out a finger, and they will crawl on. Miranda will think it is the coolest thing ever.

Result: Communicating with butterflies was much harder than with Winston. Could be that their ears are too small—or I'm just not that good at the magic part yet. Instead of butterflies, three caterpillars fell out of a tree in the playground onto Miranda's head.

Katie told Miranda there were worms in her hair. Miranda freaked out. Paula whacked her in the head with her math book. Miranda was sent home early so she could wash the worm ick out of her hair.

The Make-a-Best-Friend Plan was going to take longer than a week. I was stuck going to Bumbershoot's.

eleven

How you know you aren't at a regular doctor's office:

- Instead of crisp white walls and stiff vinyl chairs, Bumbershoot's is painted a bright purple with gold glitter trim. The chairs are covered in purple velvet.
- It smells like lavender instead of rubbing alcohol.
- In the waiting room there is a little kid who has gotten his mom's wand stuck in his ear, someone who kept sneezing bright pink glittery clouds because she'd developed an allergy to pixie dust, and a fairy whose wing is hanging at an awkward angle because she'd flown into a window.
- The "doctor" is wearing a lime green dress with a pink turban.

It was a lousy way to be spending a Saturday. I could think about six zillionty things I would rather be doing—even cleaning the bathroom would be better. I glanced over at my sister. My parents couldn't take me to Bumbershoot's because they were called away for a fairy godmother emergency. Someone's wedding would be perfect, but I was stuck with my sister.

After what seemed like forever, Doc Bumbershoot called my name. Lucinda stood up.

"You don't need to come in with me," I said.

"Of course I do. Mom will want to know what Bumbershoot has to say."

"I can tell her myself."

Lucinda sighed. She always acted like it was hard to be my sister. I knew the only reason she offered to take me was so she could stick her big nose in.

"Fine." I rolled my eyes and marched past Lucinda and into Bumbershoot's examination room.

"She hasn't gotten her fairy godmother power yet," Lucinda blurted out as soon as we walked into the room. "Everyone in our family got their powers right away. We think something might be wrong with her."

"Nothing's wrong with me," I protested.

Doctor Bumbershoot began to hum and wave her hands around in circles above my head. "I'm sensing a blockage of some sort," she said.

"I think everything's fine." I tried to avoid slapping away the doctor's hands. "I'm sure my power will show up someday. Probably in a couple weeks."

Doctor Bumbershoot rubbed a dandelion under my chin and then inspected the pollen smear closely. "Very interesting."

"What would cause a power blockage?" Lucinda asked.

"Hard to say." Bumbershoot clucked her tongue. "Ever since the Hiding there's been more of this every year. Could be that by hiding our abilities it weakens them somehow."

"But we had to go into hiding or the Humdrums would have locked us up," Lucinda said.

"It's not the Humdrums' fault, it's the fault of the fairies who pulled the tricks. Besides, all this happened a zillion years ago; things might be totally different now." I was getting sick of everyone blaming the Hiding on Humdrums.

"Or maybe they would lock us all up," Lucinda fired back.

"No one's locking anyone up. As far as they know, fairy godmothers are nothing more than a fairy tale." Bumbershoot pulled out a pair of giant sunglasses that were studded with crystals all around the frame. She put them on. It made her eyes look even larger. "I need to peek into your spirit now, Willow. It won't hurt."

"Um, okay." I tried to stay still as Bumbershoot got closer and closer until our noses were pressed together. Bumbershoot's eyes were just a couple of inches away from mine. I could feel my eyes wanting to cross as they tried to focus.

"Lord have mercy, talk about a bunch of ridiculous malarkey," a voice said from the floor. I looked down and saw a calico cat wind through Bumbershoot's legs.

"Ridiculous," I repeated, surprised. I still wasn't used to hearing animals talk. This one even had a thick Southern accent.

"I beg your pardon," Doctor Bumbershoot said, her mouth pulling down into a frown. "I know it might seem silly, but this tells me a lot. Now let me consult my books to see what we can do." She pulled down a large blue book and began to flip through the pages.

"You can hear me?" the cat said. She jumped up on the counter and peered at me with interest. "I haven't seen anyone who could talk to animals in a long time. Impressive." Her tail flicked back and forth. "I'm Louise."

I shrugged one shoulder. I jerked my head in Bumbershoot and my sister's direction, trying to signal I couldn't talk now.

The cat sat down. The tip of her tail swished around. "Buttercup, not to worry. You don't have to talk aloud. You should be able to talk to me in your head."

"One-two-three. Testing. Can you hear me?" I yelled inside my head.

"Darling, I'm sitting just a foot away. No need to bellow."

"Wow. I had no idea I could talk to you guys in my head. This is pretty cool. Can you hear everything I'm thinking?"

"I can hear pretty much everything. I think there is a way you can block your private thoughts, but that will take practice." Louise cocked her head. "Now, what on earth are you doing here telling Bumbershoot you didn't get your power when you clearly have it? In fact, you have one of the best powers. You're able to make the connection between animal and fairy. Ability to communicate like that is very powerful."

"It's a long story, but I don't want to go to sprite

school, I want to go to a Humdrum school. At least for a couple more weeks."

"Seems a tremendous shame; with a power like that, why, I'd think you'd want to yell it from the roof-tops." Louise looked over at my sister. "What in the world is wrong with that girl? Does she have ants in her pants?"

Lucinda was fidgeting in her chair, trying to get Doctor Bumbershoot's attention.

"Doctor Bumbershoot?" Lucinda pulled out some notes. "I did some research. The numbers of fairies who don't get their powers, or their powers are super weak, is getting larger all the time."

"True, but that doesn't mean there's a need to worry. Your sister is probably just fine." Bumbershoot didn't look up. She trailed a finger down the pages in the book looking for just the right spell.

"But what happens if she doesn't get one?" She held her hand over her heart.

"That girl bother you as much as she does me?" Louise asked.

"You don't know the half of it," I agreed.

"You should hack up a hairball in her shoe." Louise licked her paw and smoothed back the fur on her face.

"Now, Willow, I've got good news. I have something that should do the trick." Bumbershoot shut her book with a bang.

"Thank the Fairy Gods," Lucinda said.

Doctor Bumbershoot opened a small closet door. It was stuffed from top to bottom with all sorts of things. I could see dried herbs and flowers, stacks of folded bright fabrics, a trumpet, and what I was pretty sure was a giant Q-tip the size of a baseball bat. Bumbershoot pulled out a small paper-covered package tied shut with twine. The package gave a bump and a shiver.

"What is it?" I asked.

"It is an energy attractor. It will help the universe spot you and bring your powers."

"What if I don't want to take anything?" I was trying to see what was in the box.

"Of course she'll take it." Lucinda gave me a look. "It's important to do whatever you need to do to get your power." Lucinda nodded at Bumbershoot. "I can fly. Started first thing on my tenth birthday, even before breakfast. My sprite teacher tells me she's never seen anyone as natural as me. I suspect in another year I'll start teaching flyers in the younger classes."

"My goodness, but that girl does love to run her mouth," Louise said.

Bumbershoot held the package right in front of my face, but before I could look down to see what it was, she blew into the package and a cloud of sparkling dust flew into my face. "Try not to breathe it in," she hacked as the dust went everywhere.

I shut my eyes tight and then held my breath. Since I already had my power, would this magnet draw in too much energy? Was I about to blow up?

"Well, I'll be. That's something you don't see every day," Louise said.

I opened my eyes. I didn't feel any different. Bumbershoot was looking at me with her arms crossed in satisfaction. My sister had her mouth wide open. It had to be something big to make her be quiet. I looked into the mirror above Bumbershoot's sink and my heart stopped.

My hair was bright pink. Pink with sparkles. I touched it softly.

"Well, that should attract some attention," Bumbershoot said.

"I can't go to school like this! I'm going to Humdrum school. No one there has pink sparkling hair. No one!" I looked at Louise.

"Oh, dear. You should've said something before. It should only last about a week or so," she purred sympathetically.

"A week!"

"Don't you worry, Buttercup. The secret to being different is to revel in it. Makes people worry you're having more fun than they are." Louise sat purring next to me.

"Willow?" Lucinda said sounding impatient.

I looked up. Lucinda and Doctor Bumbershoot were standing by the door. It looked like the exam was over.

"Now, you come back and see me soon. I don't have nearly enough chances to have a nice sit-down and chat." Louise jumped down and wove through my legs. "Good luck with your power, sweetie. Don't hide it forever; it's a handy thing."

I stopped to rub Louise's ears before following my sister out into the waiting room.

"Don't look so grumpy," Lucinda said. "Mom can enchant your hair so it looks brown for the Humdrums at school. Besides, don't you want to start getting better right away?"

"I don't need to get *better*. I'm fine."

* 68 *

"You're not fine, you're"—Lucinda lowered her voice to make sure no one in the waiting room could hear us—"Humdrum."

I rolled my eyes and stomped out of Bumbershoot's waiting room. No matter what everyone around me believed, there were worse things than being Humdrum.

twelve

Things that would explain having bright pink glittery hair:

    a.   That it was my favorite color

    b.   That I was planning to try out for the circus and it was part of my costume

    c.   That I was in a rock band on the weekends

    d.   Nope, I couldn't come up with anything either

I stood outside the school and shoved the hat down farther on my head, trying to hide as much of my hair as possible. My mom tried to enchant my hair back to brown, but whatever Bumbershoot had used was super strong. It would stay brown for a few minutes and then pink strands would start popping out here and there until my whole head turned pink again. I had decided that it would be harder to explain my hair changing color while the Humdrums watched, so I was stuck going to school with a pink head.

"The hat is a mistake," Winston said. "Never try and hide who you are. That's one of my mottos."

"I told my mom I wanted a baseball cap, but this is the only hat she had." The hat was a floppy straw hat with a giant red bow around the rim. "Besides, what do you know about fashion; you don't wear any clothes."

Winston snorted through his muzzle. "I know enough to not wear that hat. Know what looks good on you, that's another motto." Winston gave me a wink.

"Who knew a dog would have so much great advice. I should start writing these down."

"That would be great." Winston's tail started to thump on the ground. He totally missed that I was joking.

"I have to go in now. They rang the bell."

"Oh. Right. Of course. Well, off you go. Education is a person's best friend, another good motto."

I watched Winston as he bounced down the street. I really needed to get a best friend who wasn't a dog.

I held my head high and walked into the school playground; maybe nobody would notice. Miranda and her friends were playing soccer. Miranda kicked the ball out of bounds and it rolled close to me. This was my chance! I dashed over before her friend Bethany could get to it and swung my leg to give the ball a kick like it had never seen before. My leg sailed right over the ball with a *whoosh* and I fell down onto my butt. Turns out playing with a real ball is different than with fairy ball. Our balls are magnetically attracted to our shoes. It's impossible to miss a kick.

"Nice. Real swift!" Bethany called out, laughing. She jogged over and bounced the ball around with her feet. Show-off. I sat on the ground. Bethany was lucky that my magic power wasn't the ability to turn her into an animal or she would be something icky like a wombat right about now.

Bethany looked down at me, her nose wrinkled up. "What's with the hat?"

I shrugged. I could feel my face burning hot with embarrassment.

"Let me try it." Bethany swiped the hat off my head before I could stop her. My hair fell down around my shoulders. Bethany had to hold her hand in front of her eyes to block the glare as the sun bounced off the glittery bits. Paula pointed at my head. Even I knew pointing was rude, and I wasn't even a Humdrum.

"Holy cow." Miranda stood staring at me with her mouth open. "Look at your hair."

I wanted to dig a hole and crawl in. Now everyone was staring at my head.

"Hey, cool!" Katie said as she walked up. She held out her hand to help me up. "I saw on TV that a bunch of movie stars are doing pink hair."

"Who has hair like that?" Bethany asked with her hands on her hips.

"Duh. You expect Madonna to call you when she changes her hair color?" Katie held up her hand to her head like it was a phone. "Bethany? Hollywood calling, we've got a style alert for you."

Miranda laughed. Bethany scrunched up her face. She was mad, but she wasn't going to say anything else. The three of them went back to playing soccer.

"Thanks," I said to Katie. I trailed my sneaker in the dirt making a pattern.

"For what?"

"You didn't really see pink hair on the TV. No one else in the world, even movie stars, would have hair like this." I ran my hand through my hair, trying to keep it down.

"Maybe not, but they might."

"I can explain. I was trying to—"

Katie shrugged. "You don't have to explain."

"You really don't want to know why my hair's this color?"

"I'm sure you have a reason." Katie looked at me. "You have a reason, don't you?"

"Sort of."

"Good enough for me." Katie fished in her book bag.

I saw a squirrel run along the top of the fence that bordered the playground. An idea snapped into my head and before I could think about it, I called out to him in my mind.

"Hey! Do you want to earn some extra nuts?" The squirrel stopped and turned, his tail twitching. I quickly explained my idea. The squirrel took off at a run and launched himself off the fence and directly onto Bethany's head. Paula and Miranda both screamed, but Bethany didn't seem to know what to do. The squirrel ran in tight circles around and around on the top of her head until her hair was knotted up like a giant beehive. By that time Bethany was spinning around smacking herself in the head. The squirrel jumped down and ran away before anyone could do anything. I called out after him that I would leave the nuts for him tomorrow after lunch. Paula and Miranda rushed over to help a hysteri-cal Bethany.

"That rat was in my hair! It was touching my hair!" Her hands tried to run through her hair but it was knotted up at least a foot high.

"I think it was a squirrel, not a rat," Paula pointed out.

"I wonder if you should call your mom. You might need shots or something," Miranda suggested.

Ha! I noticed Bethany didn't seem to find her *own* hair problems that funny.

Katie was watching where the squirrel had run through the fence. "Huh. You don't see that often. I wonder if her shampoo smells like peanut butter or something."

I shrugged. "Maybe."

"Do you want to come over to my house after school tomorrow?" Katie asked.

I looked over, surprised. "Okay."

I wasn't sure what was better, getting back at Bethany or having my first invite to a Humdrum's house. It almost made up for having bright pink hair. Almost.

thirteen

Things birds are good for:
- Eating worms so they don't get squished on the sidewalk
- Singing
- Looking pretty

You'll notice I don't list being friends with them.

Katie unlocked the front door with a key she wore on a chain around her neck. She dropped her backpack on the floor, kicked off her shoes, and took a running slide down the hall. "Mooooooooom, we're home!"

I looked down at my watch. I couldn't stay too long. I told my mom I was going to the library after school. And I did go, for about one minute before I followed

Katie home. This meant it wasn't totally a lie. Besides, my parents never would have let me come over, and this was a chance to see a real live Humdrum home up close.

I stepped inside the house carefully and looked around. It didn't look like the pictures of houses in catalogs. It wasn't as neat. It wasn't messy, but it wasn't perfect, either. There were books on the sofa and there seemed to be an art project spread over the table. My nose twitched. I smelled warm chocolate chip cookies. I would have to write this down: Humdrum homes smelled better than they looked in catalogs.

"Are you coming?" Katie was already at the top of the stairs.

I ran up the stairs after Katie, trying to notice as many things as I could as I went. She pushed open the door to her room. It was painted a bright yellow and she had posters taped on the walls. Katie had a couple of stuffed animals lined up on her bed. In the corner was a huge white birdcage. Inside a gray parrot began to bob and weave as soon as it saw Katie.

"Hello, Pretty Girl! Hello!" the bird called out. I gave it a casual nod. She certainly was friendly.

"Hi, Crackers!" Katie called back.

I spun around to look at her. "You heard her talk?" My heart sped up. Did Katie somehow have magical abilities?

"I taught her to talk," Katie said proudly. "African Grays are the most talkative of any parrot." Katie clucked at the cage and Crackers clucked back.

She was small and a dark ash gray on top with a lighter gray on her tummy. Her tail feathers were bright red. The only thing I didn't like were her feet. She had those icky bird feet that look like dried-out rubber bands with claws.

"It's rude to call someone's feet ugly. Besides, I think you have funny ears. Funny ears! Funny ears!"

"Did you hear her say that?" I asked Katie.

Katie raised an eyebrow. "She didn't say anything."

"Ha! Of course not. I was just goofing around." I laughed like I'd made a great joke. I glared at Crackers. "Don't trick me like that," I said to her.

"Finally someone can hear me really talk and it has to be you." I thought I saw Crackers roll her eyes.

"Well, you don't have to say anything."

"It's my house, I can say whatever I want."

"Fine, be that way," I shot back.

"Fine, be that way," Crackers repeated.

"So now you're going to copy whatever I say?"

"So now you're going to copy whatever I say?"

"Cut it out," I said.

"Cut it out," Crackers repeated. This bird was annoying. I was standing nose to beak with Crackers.

"Aw, you guys seems to really like each other," Katie said. "Here, I'll get her out so you can hold her."

Both Crackers and I pulled back. It didn't look like she liked the idea of getting any closer to me, either. Katie opened the cage and made the clucking sound again. Crackers fluttered and then settled on her finger. Katie pulled her out and petted the top of her feathered head.

"I'm not sure this is a good idea," I said. Crackers seemed like the kind of bird who should stay in her cage.

"Oh, she won't bite." Katie put Crackers on my shoulder. I could feel Crackers's icky toenails through my shirt.

"You better not bite," I growled in my head.

"You think I want a beak full of you?" Crackers sniffed. "I bet you would taste nasty."

"I bet you would taste just fine roasted up with mashed potatoes and gravy."

Crackers puffed up and ruffled her feathers. "You wouldn't dare."

"Drumsticks are my favorite."

Crackers began to squawk.

"She really likes you! I can tell. She hardly ever gets this excited." Katie smiled and held out her finger and Crackers jumped back on. When Katie turned her back Crackers stuck her skinny bird tongue out at me.

"So what do you want to do?" Katie asked after she clicked the cage door shut.

I was prepared. I'd spent hours last night looking through all my Humdrum notes to get ideas. I grabbed my backpack and began to pull things out. "I brought a deck of cards, and some of my sister's makeup and nail polish in case we wanted to do makeovers. I have a box of crayons and some paint. There's a ball of yarn. I can teach you how to knit." I looked up and confessed, "I can only make scarves because that's as much as my grandma taught me. It's still sort of fun."

I went back to pulling things out of the backpack. "I brought a couple of books. I wasn't sure if you would want to read together. Here's a stuffed animal I just got for my birthday, which might be kind of babyish to play with. I brought my tennis shoes in case you want to go outside." I paused to take a deep breath. I noticed Katie was staring at the pile of stuff on her bedroom floor.

"Wow."

"I might have brought too much." I decided not to show her the other things. "I wasn't sure what you would want to do." I tried to be sure to have something she would like. This was my first Humdrum invite. I wanted to do it right.

"Talk about trying too hard," Crackers cawed from the cage.

I started to chew on my thumbnail. Maybe I did overdo it. Katie had no idea how easy she had it. She was born Humdrum, she didn't have to try and figure it out as she went along.

"Do you want to make up a story? Then we can draw the pictures that go with it. I make up stories all the time. I can show you one I wrote about pirate witches."

My eyes went wide. "You mean like imagination?"

"Yeah. We can make up whatever we want."

The idea of using our imagination made me nervous. One of the reason humans didn't notice that we were fairies was because they'd lost their sense of imagination. Now the first Humdrum I was hanging out with tells me she likes to use hers all the time.

"Um, maybe we could do something else? I'm not really good at imagination stuff."

"Tell you what. Stand up," Katie said. "Then close your eyes and spin around."

"Why?"

"Because we're going to pick what to do."

I had no idea what spinning had to do with anything, but it was Katie's house, so I figured I should do what she wanted. I stood, closed my eyes, and started to spin. I hoped I wouldn't have to do this too long. I was getting dizzy.

"Okay! Now stop and point your finger," Katie yelled. I stopped and swayed, almost falling over.

"Makeovers!" Katie yelled out. I opened my eyes. My finger was pointing to the pile of makeup. "Tell you what, you do me and I'll do you, okay?"

"Okay."

"How do you want me to make you look?" Katie asked, crouching down next to me.

"I don't know. Sort of fancy, like a movie star."

"When you do me, make me look like a zombie, okay?"

"Uh, okay."

"Willow?" Katie said.

I stopped fishing through the pile of makeup and looked at her.

"I'm super glad you came over."

I felt like standing up and spinning around again. "I'm super glad you invited me."

fourteen

True or False:

    If my sister discovers that I've borrowed the tiniest amount of her makeup she'll tell me not to worry. She'll say that is what sisters are for and offer to let me have her mint-flavored ChapStick.

If you answered True, then you don't know my sister.

I hadn't had so much fun since Sasha's mom rented a dragon to come to her birthday party. And this time there was no magic.

Katie's mom came up to her room to bring us a snack. I thought she might be mad because there was makeup everywhere, but she thought we looked great! We went downstairs and pretended their hallway was a catwalk. Katie's mom, Ms. Hillegonds, got out the camera and kept yelling out, "Darling! You look fabulous!" In all the pictures we're laughing. It was the most fun ever. Ms. Hillegonds printed out one of the pictures for me to take home.

I heard a noise as I was rounding the corner to my house.

I stopped and looked around. Winston's nose was sticking through a bush.

"Winston?" I bent down to see him.

"We've got a problem."

"Why are you hiding in the bushes?"

"It's not my fault."

"What's not your fault?"

"There you are." I turned around and Lucinda was marching down the sidewalk toward me. Uh-oh. She had already seen me or I would have hidden in the bushes too.

"You are in big trouble," Lucinda said. She sounded pretty happy about the idea.

"What did I do?"

"You know."

"Is this about your makeup?"

"What about my makeup?" Her face scrunched up

✳ 85 ✳

like she was chewing on lemons. "You're not supposed to touch my stuff. I was talking about the dog in the garage."

"Dog?" I tried to act innocent.

"Someone has been sneaking it food. I found a half-eaten tuna fish sandwich."

"I'm not really fond of tuna fish," Winston whispered from the bush. "Bologna's nice. Chicken salad. Cheese is good too."

"When Mom and Dad find out you've been keeping a dog, you're going to be grounded forever." Lucinda grabbed my backpack. "I'm going to tell them about my makeup, too. Is it in here?" She started fishing around in my bag.

"Give that back!"

Lucinda held the bag out of my reach. She dug through and took out the photo of Katie and me. She stared at it. I tried to grab it out of her hands, but all it did was tear the corner off. The picture was starting to look crumpled.

"Who is that?"

"Nobody."

"Have you been hanging out with a Humdrum?" Lucinda sounded shocked. She squinted at the picture. "What's wrong with her?"

"Her name is Katie and nothing is wrong with her. She's wearing zombie makeup."

"We're not supposed to hang out with Humdrums. You know that."

"There's nothing wrong with being friends with a Humdrum."

"Nothing wrong? There are only, like, a zillion things wrong. Do you know how many rules you've broken? I can think of three at least."

"I didn't tell her I was a fairy."

"You are barely a fairy. You still don't have your power."

"Magic isn't everything," I shot back.

Lucinda whirled around and started walking toward home. "When Mom and Dad find out everything you've been up to, you're going to wish you could do magic. You're going to need to disappear."

fifteen

Things I would rather be doing other than waiting for my parents to talk to me:

    a. Let Crackers touch my face with her disgusting feet

    b. Eat lima beans even though they make me gag

    c. Roll around in poison ivy

    d. Absolutely anything else in the whole wide world

I wished I could talk to Winston, but I didn't even know where he was. I stared out my bedroom window. I hoped he was okay. Just because my stupid sister wanted to ride her bike and went snooping around the garage, everything was ruined.

I could hear my parents talking downstairs. I wasn't sure what they would do. I'd never been in this much trouble before. I wondered if they would send me away to fairy boarding school. It was somewhere in Europe. I heard it was in a giant castle that didn't have heat and the rooms were always damp. They had a mythical beast collection. I bet I'd be stuck cleaning up dragon poop every day after classes.

The only good thing about being sent away is that I wouldn't have to see my stupid sister ever again.

"Willow, come downstairs," my dad called.

I wiped my face so they couldn't tell I had been crying. There was still a bit of glitter eye shadow on my eyelid. The makeovers at Katie's felt like a zillion years ago.

I trudged down the hall toward the stairs. Lucinda was in her room. She was sitting at her desk doing her homework. I could tell she was hoping to hear me get in trouble. I made a face when I walked by.

My mom pointed to the sofa when I walked into the living room. I sat down and sank into the cushions. I wished I could sink all the way to the floor, then into the basement.

"I can explain," I said.

"Really?" Mom crossed her arms. "Let's hear what you have to say."

I wasn't really sure where to start. I stared at my feet.

"Willow Thalia Doyle, what were you thinking?" My dad always uses our entire names when he's really mad.

"I couldn't—" I started to say, but he cut me off.

"Do you know how much trouble you could be in? You've broken not only family rules, but official fairy rules."

"I know, but—."

"Not to mention, who knows what could have happened to you. What if this girl figured out you are a fairy?"

"I didn't—"

"And you realize how bad this looks if I can't get my own kids to follow the rules when my job is enforcing fairy rules?"

"I know, but—"

"Don't interrupt me when I'm talking to you." Dad paced the room.

It seemed unfair to yell at me for talking when he was asking me questions. Parents do this kind of stuff when they're really mad.

"Are you breaking every rule in this house just for fun?"

I wasn't sure what he was thinking. This was definitely not fun. I felt like I wanted to throw up.

"Willow." My mom moved in front of Dad. At least she wasn't yelling. "We have rules because we want to keep you girls safe."

"Winston never touched Lucinda. Even when she yelled at him. There was never any risk he would eat her."

Dad's face turned even redder.

"What about this girl?" He held out the picture of Katie and me.

"She's my friend."

"Honey, fairies and Humdrums can't be friends," Mom said.

"Why not?"

"Because it's too risky. We're very different. Humdrums don't understand magic. It would upset them if they knew we existed."

My dad threw his hands up in the air. "Fairies grant wishes for Humdrums, we don't become friends with them."

"Maybe we could grant wishes better if we knew them better," I said.

"So now you know how fairies should run their business?" Dad shook his head. "Why can't you be more like your sister? Lucinda seems to be able to follow the rules."

I felt my lower lip start to shake. "Can I go to my room now?"

"You better get used to that room, young lady, because you are grounded. And that isn't your only punishment. You are done with that Humdrum school as of this minute." Dad crossed his arms over his chest.

"You can't do that." I stood up and looked at my mom for help. She shook her head.

"I can and I will." Dad's face softened. "You may not believe this right now, but I'm doing this because I love you and want what's best for you. Now go up to your room."

I ran past my dad and straight upstairs. Lucinda was standing in her doorway. Her eyes were wide.

"Are you okay?" she asked quietly.

"Are you happy now? This is what you wanted."

I stormed into my room. I slammed the door, but not hard enough to make my dad come up and yell again. I threw myself onto the bed and buried my face in my pillow.

I always knew it. My parents liked my sister better than me. She was the kid they wanted. I didn't fit in anywhere.

My life was ruined. At least I could try to keep

Winston's life from being ruined too. I snuck the phone into my room and called Katie.

"Hey! I'm glad you called. I think tomorrow we should dress exactly alike. Wouldn't that be fun?" she said without even bothering to say hi.

"I won't be in school tomorrow." I sniffed.

"Are you sick?"

"No. My parents are making me go back to my regular school."

"Why?"

"Because they want me to be exactly like my stupid sister. Be glad you're an only child."

Katie was quiet on the phone. I bet she was thinking how lucky she was to have her parents who were nothing like mine.

"It'll be okay."

"It doesn't feel like it will."

"Maybe I can convince my parents to send me to school there."

"Maybe." I couldn't tell her that unless she developed a magical ability, she couldn't go to my school. "Can you do me a huge favor?"

"What do you need?"

"You know my dog, Winston? It's a long story, but

he's out in the neighborhood. Can you find him and give him some dinner? Maybe let him sleep in your yard?"

"Your parents kicked your dog out of the house?" Katie sounded shocked.

"I'm not allowed to have a dog. My sister . . . she's sort of afraid of them. I was hiding him and I got caught."

"Wow."

"Yeah. I'm grounded until at least eighth grade. I need to figure out a plan for Winston. He sort of counts on me. It might take me a couple of days to find a new home for him. Can you help me until then?"

"You bet. I'll get my dad to go outside with me. We'll find him."

Whew. I hadn't even realized I was holding my breath. "Can you tell Winston what happened? It might seem strange, but he understands a lot for a dog."

"No problem."

"I can pay you back for any dog food you have to buy." I felt better knowing Katie would look for Winston until I could help him find a new home.

"You don't have to pay me back."

"Are you sure? He eats a lot for a little dog. Oh, and be sure you don't leave any of your shoes around. He chews on them sometimes."

"I don't mind. This is the kind of thing friends do for each other."

I felt like I was going to cry all over again. "We *are* friends, aren't we?"

"Best friends."

sixteen

Which one of these things is not like the others:
a. My mom
b. My dad
c. My sister
d. Me

I scratched my knee. I had forgotten how itchy my Fairy Academy uniform could be. You would think if the school administration could enchant the entire building, they could make uniforms that didn't make you scratch all day and didn't smell like camels when they got wet. I had only been away for a bit more than a week, but it felt like I had been gone for years.

I peeked in the classroom. Our teacher, Ms. Sullivan, wasn't there yet. I had planned to wait in the hallway until class started so I wouldn't have to talk to anyone, but I had forgotten how eye-catching my pink hair was. As soon as I peeked into the classroom Adele saw me.

"Hey, Willow! Welcome back. I love your hair," Adele said. The rest of my classmates turned around to look at me.

"Your sister said you were coming back early. What happened?" Sasha asked.

"It's sort of a long story."

"What was it like?" Adele leaned in. "Was it scary?"

"No. I liked it." Both Sasha and Adele looked at me like I was speaking Elvish. "Do you guys want to hear about the Humdrums I met?"

They looked at me, blinking. "What is there to tell?" Adele asked.

"All kinds of stuff. For example, they're really not that different from us."

"Guess what? Adele got her power," Sasha said, cutting me off.

"It's no big deal." Adele blushed and pushed Sasha like she didn't want to talk about it, but I could tell she did.

"She can float!" Sasha squealed.

"You tell everybody!" Adele said, giving her another

push. They giggled. None of the fairies in my class was interested in what I had to say.

"I tell everyone because it's so cool. Go on, show her."

"Okay, but I'm not real good yet." Adele took a deep breath. "You might want to take a step back."

Sasha and I both stepped back. Adele closed her eyes. Nothing happened. Sasha was chewing on her lower lip. Adele began to shake a little bit. Sasha squealed and then pointed toward Adele's feet. She was floating two inches above the floor. Sasha was standing on her tiptoes like she wanted to take off too.

Adele opened her eyes and smiled. "I'm doing it! Can you see?"

It didn't look like Adele should float and talk at the same time. As soon as she started to speak, she began to swing back and forth. She looked out of control to me. She bumped into one of the desks and flipped over backward onto the floor.

Sasha and I ran over to help her up.

"So did you see?" Adele said.

"That's it?" I asked. Both Sasha and Adele gave me a look. "I mean, wow, that was really cool. I guess I just pictured you floating up higher."

"I will someday. I don't have the hang of it quite yet." Adele tossed her hair over her shoulder. "It takes practice."

"I can't wait until I turn ten. I hope I can float too. Wouldn't it be cool if we all got the same power? We could all float together," Sasha said.

"Yeah, cool," I said. I pictured the three of us bopping around floating like balloons.

"How are you doing?" Adele asked.

"What do you mean?"

"Your sister told my sister that you still hadn't gotten your power. She said your family is super upset and even Bumbershoot doesn't know what to do."

I rolled my eyes. My stupid sister could never keep her mouth shut. How would she like it if I told people that she hummed in her sleep?

"I'm fine."

"I've heard lots of fairies don't get their powers right away. Mine was a week after my birthday. Now that you're back, I bet it will show up. Maybe your power didn't show up because you were surrounded by Humdrums," Adele suggested.

There was a loud *pop*. Suddenly Lester the hamster

was running across the lab table in the classroom. He knocked a few glass beakers over and they hit the floor. *CRASH, CRASH, CRASH!*

POP! Lester disappeared.

POP! Lester reappeared on top of Ms. Sullivan's desk. He started running as fast as he could, his tiny claws scratching on the desk. A stack of papers went flying.

"Put him back in his cage!" someone yelled. The Van Elder twins jumped up to stand on their chairs.

POP! Lester disappeared.

"Everyone be quiet! I need to concentrate." Bartholomew closed his eyes and squinted.

"Bartholomew got his power too," Sasha explained. "He's always showing it off."

"Boys," Adele added with a sniff.

POP! Lester was in the middle of the room on the floor. He spotted me. Lester stood on his back legs and yelled at me. "Do something! If this keeps up, I'm going to bite someone. No one could blame me."

I bent down and Lester ran right into my hands. He was panting. I had forgotten how soft he was.

"Hi, Lester," I whispered into his fur. Bartholomew was looking at me and starting to scrunch up his face. "Don't you dare!" I yelled. "You aren't supposed to do magic on animals until you're in Sprite 4," I told Bartholomew.

"Yeah," Lester said. "Bite him."

"I'm not going to bite him," I said to Lester inside my head.

"Well, someone should. That boy needs biting."

"Shh! Ms. Sullivan is coming!" Milo yelled from the door and everyone scattered to their seats. I walked over to Lester's cage to put him back inside. Ms. Sullivan gave me a smile as she came into the room. She went to the cupboard to pull out our practice wands. I hated practice wands. They always broke.

"Of all the schools I could live in, I have to live here. I bet other hamsters don't have these problems," Lester grumbled.

"It can't be that bad."

"I've been purple and pink, made large, made small, and been transported here and there. Last week someone did something to my ears and they were the size of baseballs. I looked like a hamster Dumbo." Lester fluffed his cedar shavings, making himself a nest for a nap.

I snickered.

"It wasn't funny. I'm a hamster. My largest concern should be if I'm spending enough time on my wheel. I shouldn't be worried about being pink." He looked at me. "It looks like you should worry more about being pink yourself."

I put Lester back in his cage and sat down in my seat. I pulled out my textbook. Ms. Sullivan stopped by my desk and handed me a bright polka-dotted envelope. I tore it open and pulled out a note.

> *Willow—*
>
> > *Always remember that wishes keep their magic as long as you remember to believe.*
>
> > > *Love, Grandma*

It wasn't that I didn't want to believe, but I didn't see how things could ever be right.

The wand on my desk had a crack down the side and was held together by black tape. I sighed. Sasha and Adele were sitting in front of me, whispering back and forth. The Van Elder twins were giggling and trying to get Bartholomew to pay attention to them. They were boy crazy. Bartholomew was talking to Milo. He was probably planning to do something to Lester again. Milo was picking his nose when he thought no one was looking.

I slumped down in my seat. Nothing had changed, except for me.

seventeen

Advantages of being grounded:
- You don't have to worry about getting your school clothes dirty playing.
- It doesn't matter if it's raining because you can't play outside.
- You aren't allowed to hang out with your best friend anyway.
- There is lots of time to get your homework done.

I sharpened my pencil. I liked the way pencil shavings smell. It helped me think. My sister liked to use a fancy fountain pen, but I always spilled the ink. I had to write a report for school on my time at Riverside and what sort of wishes I'd seen while I was there. Miranda wished for straight hair. Granting a hair wish seemed boring.

I chewed on the eraser and thought some more. One wish would be to make Katie an astronaut. Even though that was her wish, I wasn't sure it was a good idea. She would miss her family out in space.

That was the tricky thing about wish-granting. Just because someone wished for it didn't make it a good wish.

My paper was all smudged from where I had written things down and erased them. I was going to have to start all over again. This was going to take forever. I crumpled the paper and looked out the window.

Something small and black bounced up by the hedge, then disappeared.

Huh?

I stared at the hedge, but nothing happened. It must have been my imagination. Then suddenly—*BOING*—the small black body bounced into the air and then disappeared.

Winston!

I ran downstairs and out into the yard. "Winston?"

"Over here!" He bounced up again. I crouched next to the hedge and rubbed his muzzle.

"Are you okay? Did Katie explain everything?"

"She did. She says you don't have to worry. You won't be grounded forever."

"It's only going to feel like forever. Besides, even when I'm not grounded I'm still not going to be allowed to be her friend. Instead of granting wishes I need someone to grant mine," I said. Winston leaned against me so that we were pressed together.

"What would you wish for?" he asked.

"I'd need an army of fairy godmothers I have that many wishes. I would wish I could go to school with Katie. I'd wish you could stay with me. I'd wish my sister would disappear."

"Shhh!"

"I know I shouldn't say it, but she drives me nuts."

Winston growled. "No, I meant shhh, here she comes." Winston backed up so he was farther in the bushes.

I turned to see Lucinda sneaking up on me. "What are you doing out here?"

"I'm allowed to be in the yard."

Lucinda peered into the bushes. She was so nosy.

"Isn't there some homework you need to be doing or something?" I asked, standing in front of her.

"You better not be doing anything you're not supposed to. You're in a lot of trouble already." Lucinda put her hands on her hips.

"Just because you want to be perfect doesn't mean I have to be."

"I'm not perfect."

"*I* know that." I stuck my hands on my hips. We were nose to nose.

"I try to help you, but I don't know why I bother. You're impossible." Lucinda shrunk down and flew past my head. I waved her away and she buzzed off.

"You're not supposed to fly outside," I yelled after her.

I waited a minute to make sure she was really gone. I could hear Winston rustling in the bushes.

"Do you have any sisters, Winston?"

"Yeah, but we all went to different homes. We don't keep in touch. Dogs make lousy letter-writers."

"GOTCHA!" a voice yelled from the yard next door. Winston jumped. I peeked over the hedge. It was Kevin, the Humdrum kid who lived next door.

He was dancing around his backyard with a glass jar in his hand.

"What do you have?" I called out.

Kevin came over to the hedge and peeked through the bushes. "My dad said they don't exist this time of year, but I told him he was wrong!"

"What doesn't exist?"

"Fireflies." He held out the glass jar. He had punched holes in the top of the lid and there was a handful of grass and twigs inside.

There was one more thing in the jar. It flew from top to bottom, side to side, bouncing off the glass. But it wasn't a firefly.

It was my sister.

eighteen

If your know-it-all sister is captured in a jar by the neighbor Humdrum kid you might feel:
   a. Happy
   b. Excited
   c. Really scared and like you might throw up

Even though she drove me crazy and I always said I wanted to get rid of her, the answer was *c*.

Kevin held the jar out so it was right next to my face. I peered inside. Winston jumped up and down at my feet, trying to get a look.

"Lucinda?" I whispered. The yellow glowing creature started bouncing around faster. Yep, it was my sister. If she thought *I* was in trouble, wait until Mom and Dad found out she had been flying around in public. She started to ping against the glass. I couldn't tell because she was really small, but I was pretty sure she had her tiny hands on her tiny hips and was telling me to stop asking stupid questions and do something.

"Isn't it cool? I'm going to keep it in my room. It will be like a night light." Kevin grabbed the jar back. He hugged it close. He was six. Six-year-old boys like bugs and worms. They're sort of yucky like that.

"Maybe you should let it go," I said.

"No way." He stepped back. "You can't make me."

"Well, it can't live in a jar forever."

"I don't care if it lives. I'm going to feed it to my lizard anyway."

Lucinda went completely still in the jar.

"You're going to let a lizard eat her?"

Kevin laughed when he saw my face. Winston whimpered and his tail dropped down.

"Yeah. Do you want to watch?" He made a bunch of disgusting chewing sounds.

"No!" I felt like running around the yard screaming, but I knew that wouldn't help. "I bet your lizard wouldn't like this firefly. It could make your lizard sick."

"Are you kidding? Godzilla loves bugs. I feed him crickets every day."

"Maybe Godzilla would rather have a carrot or something. Being a vegetarian is really cool."

"I hate vegetables." He frowned.

"What if this bug has a family? Wouldn't you feel bad?"

"Nope."

There was no point in trying to argue with a boy. They're hopeless. "Give me that!" I tried to snatch the jar out of his hand.

He jumped back in surprise. He almost fell down, but he managed to stay on his feet.

"Hey! You can't do that." He stepped back so he was out of my reach.

"I need that bug," I told him. "I happen to like that particular bug. At least some of the time." I mentally went through my piggy bank. "I can give you five dollars for the bug."

"No."

I could hear Lucinda buzzing. She knew I got Humdrum money from Grandma for my birthday. There was no need to yell, I just wanted to see if he would take less.

"How about ten dollars?"

"No way. Get your own bug." Kevin ran back to his house, taking my sister with him.

I always wanted Lucinda to disappear, but I never imagined her being fed to a lizard. She might be able to turn back when he opened the jar to feed her to the lizard, but if she wasn't fast it would be all over. I didn't know how quick she could change and I was pretty sure she wasn't good at doing magic under pressure. I couldn't take a chance.

"Winston, I need you stay here and watch that house. If you see Kevin with a lizard I need you to bark like crazy. I've got to go get Mom and Dad."

They'd know what to do. They would work some magic and would rescue Lucinda. I was sure of it.

nineteen

You sister is about to be eaten alive by a lizard named Godzilla. You tell your parents and they:

a. Rush to save her life while telling you what a wonderful kid you are

b. Ask you to tell them the story again so they have all the information

c. Assume you are making the whole thing up

Can you guess what happened?

I ran into the living room, screaming at the top of my lungs for my parents. They sat on the sofa while I spilled the whole story. I told them about Kevin and Godzilla. I explained how I tried to get the jar back. I figured they would say thanks to me for trying to save her. After all, they were crazy about Lucinda.

But they just looked at each other.

"I think I know what this is about," Dad said.

"What are you going to do? Can you transport the whole jar out of there? Or maybe some kind of sleeping spell so that we could sneak into the house and get her?" My dad was great at all kinds of spells. I knew he would come up with something good.

"We're not going to do anything," Mom said. She picked up her knitting and started work on a sock. She nodded at another set of needles on the couch and they floated up in the air and started knitting the matching sock.

What? I looked back and forth between my parents.

"Enough storytelling for one day. If you keep this up you'll be grounded for another week," Dad said.

"I'm not telling a story." I threw my arms up in the air. "This isn't like the dog."

"Or the time you told us your sister ran away and instead you had her locked in the garage?"

It wasn't fair for them to bring that up. That was forever ago. Like last year.

"It is against the rules for your sister to fly outside. Sprites aren't able to practice that level of magic without supervision. It's too risky."

✧ 113 ✧

"Lucinda knows she'd be in big trouble if she did something like that." My mom's knitting needles clacked together. "Your sister wouldn't break a rule like that. You know that as well as we do."

"I know you're mad at your sister, but trying to get her in trouble is wrong," Dad said.

"You don't believe me?"

"Lucinda told us she was going to the library to study."

"But she didn't. Or maybe she thought she would fly there. I know she's not at the library. She's in a jar on Kevin's desk and he's going to feed her to a lizard! One named Godzilla!" I couldn't believe my parents didn't believe me. Boy, talk about a bad time for your parents to think you were making something up.

"Enough. Go up to your room and do your homework." My dad went back to reading his paper.

I stood there. They had to believe me.

"Go on, I'll call you when dinner is ready," Mom said.

How could she think about dinner when her older daughter was about to be a glittery reptile snack?

"But Mom—"

"Go on."

I ran upstairs and went into my parents' room.

I yanked open the closet door and rummaged in the boxes they had stacked on the floor. I pulled out my dad's binoculars and ran into my room.

I dove across my bed and landed in front of my window. I put the binoculars up to my eyes and tried to focus on the house next door. I scanned across the windows. THERE! It was Kevin's bedroom. There was a giant poster of monster trucks on the wall. I could see his desk. On top of the desk was a large aquarium with a lizard. Godzilla was sitting on his hot rock, flicking his tongue. Right next to his aquarium was the jar with my sister in it.

If my parents weren't going to do anything, then I would have to. First I needed a plan. Lucky for my sister, I knew just the person who could think of one.

I snuck back down the stairs with my backpack and slid along the hallway past the living room. I held my breath as I went by, but my parents didn't see me. For once it was good to be the kid they didn't notice.

I ran out into the yard, calling for Winston. He bounded up.

Winston gave a salute and then sat down at my feet. "No one has left the house. No signs of the lizard.

The dad has come home. The mother is cooking ham-burgers for dinner. It smells to me like she's overcook-ing them, but I can't tell from out here."

"I'm not worried about the burgers."

"Roger that. Waste of good hamburger, though. Never undercook, never overcook. That's another motto."

"My parents don't believe me. I'm going to have to rescue Lucinda myself."

"How are you going to do that?"

"I don't know." I was getting desperate.

"That sounds like a problem."

"I'm going to fix it, but we're going to need everyone who can help."

"I'll help." Winston sat up straighter and thrust his chin out. He looked ready for battle. I bent down and hugged him.

"I need you to get additional reinforcements. Go to Doctor Bumbershoot's and get her cat, Louise."

"Cat?" Winston's lip curled up like he had tasted bad bologna.

"You'll like Louise. Or at least try not to chase her. Then both of you go to school and get Lester the ham-ster. Meet back here as soon as you can."

"What are you going to do?"

"I'm going to get a plan."

Winston held out his paw and we shook on it before running off in opposite directions.

All I could do was hope that Godzilla didn't eat an early dinner.

twenty

If you are looking for a best friend, you want one who has:
   a. lots of cool stuff you can play with.
   b. a mom who makes homemade cookies when you come over.
   c. a fancy house.
   d. a great sense of imagination and can come up with a great plan to rescue your sister who is trapped in á jar and might be eaten by a lizard.

Absolutely *d*!

I ran all the way to Katie's house. I knocked on the door and hoped her mom wouldn't notice how sweaty I was.

"Willow! How nice to see you."

"Hi-can-I-talk-to-Katie?" All my words came out in a big rush.

"We're going to have dinner soon."

"I-promise-it-won't-take-long." I chewed on my bottom lip. "Please? It's important."

"Is everything okay?"

"It's sort of best friend stuff."

"I wouldn't want to get in the way of best friend stuff. Go ahead and run up to her room."

I flew up the stairs and into Katie's room. Katie was sitting on top of her steamer trunk wearing cowboy boots. She was writing in her notebook.

"Hey! I'm making up a story about a rancher and his trusty steed, Black Star." Katie patted the trunk before looking up at me. "I thought you were grounded."

"I wanted to know if you could help me with an imagination thing."

"You do? I thought you hated pretend stuff."

"I don't hate it. I'm just not very good at it."

"Okay. Jump up on the bed. You can help me write the bit about the rancher going on a cattle drive."

"I need your help imagining something else."

Katie stared at me. I had the feeling she could tell it was more important than pretend cowboys or pirates.

She slid off the trunk onto the floor where she could sit cross-legged.

"How can I help?"

"Imagine what you would do if you had to rescue a fairy princess who was being kept in a high castle. The evil ogre plans to feed her to his dragon." I looked at my watch. "And he plans to do it pretty soon."

"Do we have an army or anything?"

I thought about it. "Sort of a small army."

Katie sat tapping her pen against her mouth. I could tell she was thinking, so I kept quiet. "All right, most rescue plans have three stages. Distraction, breaking in, and then breaking back out."

"Okay." I wondered if I should write this down.

"Distraction can be the hard part. We have to do something to get the ogre's attention. Blowing stuff up works pretty good."

"I'm not sure about explosives." My dad kept a lot of stuff in the garage, but I didn't think we had any dynamite. Even if we did, I'd be in a lot of trouble if I used it.

"Then we need something else pretty splashy. Something that the ogre can't ignore. The break-in part of the plan is harder. Can anyone in our army scale the wall of the castle once the ogre is distracted?"

"I don't think so." I was pretty sure Winston would be afraid of heights. I chewed on my lip and then noticed Crackers in her cage. "Wait a minute. We might have someone who could get up high."

"Perfect!" Katie jumped up and grabbed a sheet of blank newsprint from her craft table. "Grab some markers, we need to draw a diagram. Don't worry about step three. The getaway is the easiest part; you run really fast."

While Katie started to draw I looked over at Crackers's cage.

"I need to ask you a favor," I said inside my head.

Crackers ruffled her feathers and gave a sniff. "Me? Do you need something to go with your mashed potatoes?"

"I'm sorry about that."

"Hmmff."

"It's a matter of life and death." Crackers bopped her head back and forth. She was thinking about it. "You could be a hero," I said, "like an eagle."

"An eagle?" She spread her wings. "If it's a case of life and death, I suppose I could help this one time."

We had just enough time to finish the plan before Katie's mom called her for dinner. I went downstairs, but when we got to the door I stopped short and smacked my forehead.

"I forgot my bag in your room," I said, crossing my fingers behind my back so the lie wouldn't count.

"I'll get it for you," Katie said.

I grabbed her arm. "No, I got it." I dashed past her up the stairs and into the room. I flung the door to Cracker's cage open. "Okay, come on. You can hide under my shirt or in my bag."

Crackers ruffled her feathers. "I don't think so."

"We don't have time for this; I have to get you out of here."

"I won't be able to breathe under there."

I wanted to scream. I would have grabbed her and stuffed her under my shirt except I knew she'd make a fuss. "I need to get you out of here without Katie seeing. I suppose you have a better idea?" I said through my teeth.

"As a matter of fact, I do. Open the window." Crackers motioned to Katie's bedroom window with her foot. "I'll meet you outside."

I shut my mouth with a click. The bird wasn't so birdbrained after all. I smiled. This plan was going to work. It had to.

twenty-one

Things to bring on a rescue mission:

1. A plan
2. Binoculars
3. A diagram
4. The very best friends you can find

I wished I could have brought Katie to help with putting her plan into action. I bet she would be great on a rescue mission, but I didn't know how to get her help without explaining how my sister ended up in a jar in the first place. I lay in the grass outside Kevin's house and looked through the binoculars. Whew. Lucinda was still there. It was making me nervous how Godzilla kept flicking his tongue in her direction. It was like he was trying to taste her. Kevin poked his finger into the aquarium at Godzilla. There were no grown-ups to be seen. The coast was clear.

Winston was lying on the ground next to me. His back legs spread out behind him. He had gotten the reinforcements I'd asked for. Louise was sitting quietly with just the tip of her tail swishing back and forth. Lester kept turning around quickly to see if Louise was sneaking up on him. Crackers was perched in the tree.

"Fuzzy muffin, you don't need to worry. I haven't eaten a mouse in years. I like my food cooked to perfection. I don't eat things that still have their legs." Louise patted Lester on top of his head with one white paw. Lester looked like he was ready to have a heart attack. He was a very high-strung hamster. I hoped he was up to the mission.

"I am not a mouse." Lester sounded offended.

"I don't eat whatever you might be, sugar cheeks." Louise licked her paws with a dainty tongue.

"Is everyone clear on the plan? We can go over the diagram again." I had Katie's map spread out on the ground. "Once we get you up there, we need to get you to push the jar out of the window. It's risky, but our only option. I'll catch it and then we all run for it."

"Shouldn't I have some kind of protective gear? Like a helmet?" Lester asked. "What if she drops me?"

"I won't drop you," Crackers said. "I'm like an eagle."

Lester rolled his eyes. "Can't I ride in my ball?"

"There are no places for Crackers to hold on to your ball," I said.

"Plus it's too heavy," Crackers said. "I could break a nail." She looked over her feet.

"I bet an eagle could carry one little ball," Lester grumbled.

"Drop it, you two. Keep your focus on the mission," Winston ordered.

Through the window I could see Kevin pick up the jar with Lucinda in it and give it a shake.

"Okay, we've got to go now. He's touching the jar. Is everyone ready?"

I stuck my hand out. Winston put his paw on top. Louise daintily placed her paw on top of his. Lester gave a sigh, but climbed up my leg and out on my arm to put his tiny paw onto hers. Crackers fluttered down and perched on the top of our pile.

"To victory!" I cried.

"To victory!" everyone yelled out.

. . . . .

EILEEN COOK

Louise was the one who came up with the idea for a distraction. I had planned on having Winston and Louise have a fight, because boys liked fights. They were always whacking each other on the playground. My only other idea was to cover myself with ketchup and let it look like Winston was eating me alive. Louise said a distraction didn't have to be loud or yucky, that people were more often surprised by something beautiful than something ugly. I hid in the bushes. I kept the binoculars focused on Kevin's bedroom. Lester and Crackers were ready to go when they heard the signal.

"None of my friends better see me," Winston grumbled.

"Buttercup, they would think you were the luckiest dog in the world to dance with me. Ancient Egyptians worshipped cats, and they were smart enough to build the pyramids." Louise leaped up onto the picnic table. Winston tried to make the same jump, but hit the side of the table and fell back to the ground.

"I meant to do that," he said.

"'Course you did." Louise wriggled her whiskers. It looked like she was trying to keep from laughing.

Winston jumped onto the bench and from there onto the table.

"Everyone ready?" I met their eyes and they nodded one by one. I crossed my fingers. "Okay, Winston, raise the alarm."

Winston began howling. As soon as Kevin appeared at the window, he stopped howling. Winston stood up on his hind legs and made a slight bow at Louise. She stood up on her hind feet and they began waltzing.

"One, two, three . . . ," Louise said counting out a tempo. "Think of it as a box."

"That's what I'm doing," Winston said. They spun around the table.

"Whoever taught you ballroom dancing should be shot."

"Look, Miss Fancy Cat, if you weren't trying to lead, maybe I wouldn't be stepping on your paws."

Kevin's mouth fell open. He rubbed his eyes and looked again. He opened the window and leaned out. *Come on, come get a closer look*, I thought. He couldn't ignore this, could he? It was a dancing cat and dog!

Finally, Kevin left the window and I followed him with the binoculars.

"He's left the room! Crackers, GO! Go right now!"

Crackers stretched her wings and took a couple of deep breaths.

"Are we sure there isn't another option?" Lester asked. I think he was going to say something else, but all he got out was a tiny *EEP* sound as Crackers took off with him in her claws.

Crackers's wings flapped hard, but it didn't look like she was going to get much more than five feet above the ground.

"You need to lay off the carrots," Crackers huffed. "Spend more time on the wheel."

Lester didn't say anything back. He had his eyes squeezed shut and his tiny paws covering them. I held my breath.

"I'm an eagle, I'm an eagle," Crackers chanted. She kept flapping her wings and finally she was starting to gather enough speed to get up high.

Crackers reached the window and dropped Lester onto the desk. He sat there with his paws still over his eyes.

"Lester!" He was either too scared or too far away, and wasn't listening to me.

The back door flew open. Kevin skidded out onto the patio with his parents right behind him. Instantly Winston and Louise stopped dancing and sat still on top of the picnic table. Winston scratched his ear with his back paw.

"There they are!" Kevin pointed at them.

Kevin's mom and dad looked at Winston and Louise and then at each other.

"They were dancing. They were."

"I need to finish making dinner," Kevin's mom said.

"No wait. Maybe if there was some music." Kevin started humming.

Louise yawned.

"I think someone's had too much candy," his dad said. "All that sugar isn't good for you." His parents went back inside.

Upstairs Lester was still huddled on top of the desk, shaking. Crackers perched next to him and whacked him with her wing. It seemed to be exactly what he needed. He stood up and shook it off. He then ran over and sniffed all around the jar. Lester stood on his hind legs and pushed the jar. It teetered back and forth and then fell over onto its side.

"I saw you dancing," Kevin said to Winston and Louise. When he turned to go back in the house, Louise let out a yowl. He turned around and she and Winston started to dance again.

"Are you up for trying the tango? I love the tango," Louise said.

"I'm going to get my camera!" Kevin ran inside.

"Uh-oh," Winston said. "He's not sticking around to watch."

"I knew we should have tangoed."

All of us turned to look back at the window.

"HURRY!" I urged Lester in my mind.

Lester put his front paws on the jar and began to roll it toward the end of the desk. It began to roll faster. I held my breath.

The jar rolled up to the window and then . . . stopped.

"Oh, heavens, it's stuck on the sill." Louise closed her eyes. "I can't look."

Lester backed up and ran full speed at the jar. I could hear Winston gasp. I wanted to close my eyes like Louise, but I couldn't. Lester hit the jar and it flew up over the sill and out the window. He was running so hard that he ran right out the window too!

I leapt forward and dived under the window, my arms outstretched. I caught the jar in both hands. Lester was still falling, all four legs spinning madly in the air. I got ready to try to catch him, too.

"Gotcha!" Crackers swooped down and snatched Lester as he fell, lifting him back up into the air. I let out the breath I'd been holding.

"What the heck?" Kevin leaned out his window.

"Run for it!" I yelled.

I took off through the yard. Winston and Louise were right at my heels and Crackers, with Lester in her claws, flew overhead. We all skidded around the corner. I flung open the door to the garage and yanked it closed once everyone was inside.

I leaned against the door, panting. I held on to the jar. My sister buzzed and bounced against the glass.

"That was the most fun I've had in years!" Lester crowed. "I can't believe I've been happy wandering around in that ball. Flying is amazing!"

I twisted the top of the jar off and my sister flew out. There was a small *pop* and Lucinda was standing there. She was shaking. She had a bruise on her elbow and a small cut above her eye. Her lower lip started to tremble and her eyes filled with tears. I swallowed. I felt like I could cry too. Lucinda opened her mouth to say something, but stopped. Instead she took a step forward and threw her arms around me. I hugged her right back.

"You're the best sister ever," Lucinda said.

I smiled. She wasn't too bad either. At least some of the time.

"Nothing like family," Winston said. "That's another one of my mottos."

twenty-two

Lucinda is:

   a. A know-it-all

   b. A tattletale

   c. Stuck-up

   d. My sister, and I love her. If anyone feeds her to a
      lizard, it will be me. No one else is going to hurt
      her as long as I'm around.

   e. All of the above

When you are talking about sisters, they are almost
always all of the above.

"Are you okay?" I asked.

"I think so." Lucinda looked around the garage at
our rescue group. "Hey, that's the dog you were hiding,

and Bumbershoot's cat." She bent down to take a closer look. "Is that the rat you had all summer?"

"Rat?!" Lester huffed. "Talk about ungrateful."

"Lester's a hamster," I said. "He's sort of sensitive on the subject." I pointed to Crackers, who was perched on top of my bike handlebars. "This is Crackers. She belongs to my friend Katie."

"Your Humdrum friend?" she asked. "How did you train all of them to do this?"

"I didn't train them."

"Then how in the world did you do it?"

"Can you keep a secret?" I asked. Lucinda nodded. I took a deep breath. "I asked them. That's my power. They understand me. I understand them."

Lucinda's eyes opened wide. "Holy cow! Are you kidding me? Communicating with animals is, like, the most important power you can get." She looked me up and down. "Are you sure you have it?"

"Yes, I'm sure."

"Don't get mad, I just asked." She crossed her arms and stared down at Winston.

"Why is she looking at me like that?" Winston asked. He took a couple steps back.

"Did you see that? He just moved!" Lucinda gave a small jump.

"He wants to know why you're staring at him. It's freaking him out."

"Can he hear me? I'm trying to communicate with him." Lucinda squinted and tried to send mental waves to Winston.

"If you want him to hear you, then you have to say something," I said.

"You don't have to talk out loud," Lucinda pointed out.

"Yeah, but this is my power. He can understand you when you talk, but he can't read your thoughts. And you can't understand him at all."

"You don't have to be mad. I think it's great you can do this. Can you imagine what would have happened to me if you hadn't been there?" Lucinda's lower lip started to shake again. "We are family; if you have the power to communicate with animals, then I probably have some of it too. I just never tried before."

Lucinda had stopped trying to send messages to Winston. Now she was bending down, holding Louise's face in her hands and staring into her eyes.

"I'm a lady, but if she doesn't let go of me soon I'm

going to scratch one of those buggy staring eyes right out of her head," Louise warned.

"You can't handle the power you have, you shouldn't try mine," I said. I whacked her arm so she would let go of Louise.

"What are you talking about? I fly fine."

"You flew right into a jar. I wouldn't call that fine." I crossed my arms.

"Flying outside was a mistake. All I'm saying is that if either of us has the power to talk to animals, I would think it would be me. I'm the top of my sprite class. Besides, I'm the oldest."

I gave a snort sound and then looked over at Winston. I turned my head to the side. "Did you hear that?"

Lucinda's head spun around so she could see Winston. "I heard something."

"HA! He didn't say anything." I smiled.

Lucinda's eyes narrowed. "Don't be such a baby."

"I'm not a baby." I pushed her.

"Then stop acting like one!" She shoved me back.

"I'll stop when you stop being such a know-it-all," I yelled and shoved a bit harder this time. Lucinda pulled my hair. I jabbed my elbow in her ribs.

The door to the garage flew open and our dad was

standing there. Mom was right behind him. "What in the world is going on in here?" Dad bellowed.

"It's her fault!" Lucinda and I said at the same time. We pointed at each other.

"Can someone explain why our garage is a zoo?" Dad asked, looking at the lineup of animals along the wall.

Winston took a step forward and held out his front paw. "Sir, I don't believe we've been formally introduced."

"Look at the dog! How sweet." My mom bent down and shook his paw.

"I wasn't really going for sweet, but I'll take it." Winston licked her hand.

"They're my friends," I said. Louise wound around my legs, purring.

"Is that the school gerbil?" Dad asked.

"Hamster!" Lester said with a shake of his head. "Can no one in your family correctly identify an animal?" He threw his tiny paws in the air.

"Willow can talk to them," Lucinda blurted out. "That's her power."

"That girl couldn't keep her mouth shut if she had a roll of duct tape and a stapler," Louise said.

Mom and Dad both turned to face me. So much for keeping things secret.

"Lucinda was flying outside! I had to rescue her because you didn't believe me."

My parents stopped looking at me and faced Lucinda. Her face flushed bright red.

"Okay, everyone inside." My dad opened the door that connected to the house.

Lucinda's shoulders slumped. She wasn't used to being in trouble.

Winston cleared his throat. "Hate to be a bother, but is there any chance of getting a snack? All this rescue and family drama has made me hungry."

twenty-three

What will your parents focus on?

a. That you rescued your sister from being eaten alive or having to spend the rest of her life in an old jelly jar that smells like raspberries (which she hates).

b. That you didn't tell the whole truth (which is not the same as lying. It is more like telling the truth late.)

My sister couldn't handle being in trouble. We hadn't even gotten all the way inside before she confessed everything. She was never going to make it as a spy. She couldn't even keep a secret when it was in her best interest. We sat side by side on the sofa while Dad paced back and forth asking questions about what happened.

"Lucinda, what were you thinking? You know you should never fly outside without a fairy supervisor," my dad said.

"I, I, I . . ." my sister stuttered. "I needed to practice. There's going to be a flying test at school."

"Do you realize what could have happened if someone had seen you?" Dad put his hands on his hips. His face was the dark red color that meant he was really mad. "Did you even think how what you were doing was a risk for every fairy?"

Lucinda's lower lip started to shake. "I'm sorry." She started to hiccup, which she only did when she was really upset. "I just wanted to do well on my test." She sniffed. "You always say I'm your gold-star girl. I didn't want to let you down."

Dad slumped into his big leather chair. "You *are* my gold star-girl." He looked at me. "You both are."

Mom sat between us and put her arms around both of us. "We're lucky you girls are okay. That's what is most important."

"Willow and her magic saved my life," Lucinda said.

"Why didn't you tell us you got your power, Willow?" Dad asked.

Uh-oh. I still wasn't out of trouble. I had been hoping

they might forget about this part and we could focus on how I saved my sister.

"You wouldn't let me go to Humdrum school if I had my power. Then you were mad at me about the dog, and then you didn't believe me about Lucinda."

"Why is it so important that you go to Riverside?"

I shrugged. It was hard to explain. "I like the Humdrums."

Mom and Dad exchanged a look. "We all like the Humdrums. Helping them is our job," Dad explained. "Liking them doesn't mean that we are friends with them. We're too different."

"But I fit in better with the Humdrums."

"You have lots of friends at the academy," Mom said.

I sighed. "I have friends, but I don't have a *best* friend. And everyone always compares me to Lucinda. I always hear 'Your sister's so graceful, she never falls down the stairs knocking everyone down. Lucinda never broke her practice wands. Lucinda never accidently spilled an entire bottle of pixie dust and turned a whole cage of mice into unicorns.'"

"I forgot about those unicorns. Remember how Mr. Keeter was running around trying to herd them all

together and he kept falling?" Lucinda asked, while trying not to laugh.

"I can't forget because everyone always reminds me." I
covered my eyes with my hands. Now I felt like crying all
over again. "I like Humdrum school. I like my friend Katie.
It doesn't matter to me if she was fairy or Humdrum. If it
weren't for her, I never would have figured out how to save
Lucinda. The rescue plan was all her idea. And Katie likes
me just the way I am. Magic or no magic."

"We like you just the way you are too," my mom
whispered in my ear.

"Come here," Dad said. I stood and walked over to
his chair. He gave me a big hug. I buried my face in his
sweater. He always smells like fresh air and Christmas
trees. I think that's why his hugs are so great. "If we ever
made you feel like you came in second, then we owe
you an apology. You're the only Willow this family has.
One of a kind."

I hugged my dad even harder. Someone tapped my
shoulder and I turned around. Lucinda was standing
there.

"I might not break any wands, but I also never saved
anybody either. You're the best sister in the whole world.
Humdrum or fairy."

Then we were all hugging. One big giant Doyle family hug.

I caught sight of Crackers at the window. She wasn't flying. She was just standing there, except there was nothing to stand on. I ran over and looked out. Crackers was perched on Lester's head. Lester was standing on Louise, who was standing on top of Winston. They were all swaying back and forth and everyone tried to keep their balance.

"We wanted to check on how things were going," Lester said, his foot sliding down the side of Louise's face.

"Everything's fine." I smiled from ear to ear. "Better than fine, even."

"Tell your friends they don't have to wait outside," my mom said.

"They don't?"

"How can we celebrate your sister's big rescue without inviting everyone who helped?"

And just like that, it was a party.

twenty-four

Chances you'll lose something:
- If it is something small, not important, and you don't need it—almost no risk.
- If it is something you absolutely need and you'll be in big trouble if it's gone—almost certainly going to disappear.

The next morning, my mom tapped on my door to let me know it was time to get up for school. Winston was still snoring. Last night my parents decided he could stay. I finally had a dog of my very own! I had to promise to walk him every day, clean up after him, and be responsible for his food.

Winston had to promise not to eat my sister.

I scrambled out of bed and washed up. When I got

back to my room, I couldn't find my school uniform anywhere. It wasn't in the closet or on my chair. It wasn't even in the pile of clothes at the bottom of my closet. I looked in the hamper, too, but all I could find were my smelly socks.

I woke up Winston. "Did you bury my school clothes outside?"

"No. Of course not." He yawned.

"Are you sure?" I put my hands on my hips.

"Yeesh. I bury one shoe in one yard and now I always get blamed. Yes, I'm sure I didn't take your uniform." Winston grabbed the blanket in his mouth and pulled the covers back up over his head.

"It's no fair you get to sleep all day," I said.

"It's no fair I don't have opposable thumbs," Winston said. "If I had thumbs I could make my own sandwiches. Life isn't fair. Now run off and have a good day at school."

Downstairs, Mom was making my favorite ginger-bread pancakes. As soon as my dad would finish one, she would point her finger at his plate and, *POP*, a fresh hot pancake would appear. Even my perfect sister had syrup smeared on her chin.

I slid into my seat and a pancake immediately appeared on my plate. "Mom, I can't find my uniform."

"You can wear that to school," she said, bustling around the kitchen.

"You look nice," my sister added.

"But we're supposed to wear our uniforms. If we don't wear it, we get checks on our behavior sheet." I already had a few checks for other things. I had gotten two for the time I accidentally tripped Milo in the playground.

"You're not going to the fairy academy. There isn't a uniform at Humdrum—I mean, Riverside Elementary," my dad said, sticking another bite of pancake in his mouth.

I dropped my fork on the plate. Mom sat down next to Dad. They were both smiling. I was afraid to say anything in case I'd misunderstood them.

"Your mom and I talked about it last night after you went to bed. Your grandmother thinks there are a lot of advantages of you going to Humdrum school, for you and maybe for all of us. You'll go to Riverside the rest of this year. What you said last night makes a lot of sense. It seems there is a lot you can learn from the Humdrums and there's certainly a lot we can learn from you."

"Really?!"

Mom and Dad both nodded. This was great. This was better than great. This was super, amazing, holy moly great! This was even better than gingerbread pancakes. I jumped up. I wanted to go to school right now.

"Hang on. There's still plenty of time for breakfast. Besides there are also some rules we have to go over."

I've noticed that even when your parents do something great there are rules. It's like they don't want you to have too much fun all at once. I sat down in my chair.

Dad rattled off the list, counting off each of the rules on his fingers. "Rule one: absolutely no magic at school. None. Zero.

"Rule two: You can't tell anyone, even your best friend, that you're a fairy.

"Rule three: You have to agree to go for magical training on the weekends so you can keep up with your fairy classmates.

"Rule four: At the end of the year, you are going to have to write a paper about what you've learned from the Humdrums to share with the kids at the fairy academy.

"Rule five: No more keeping secrets from your mom and me." My dad waved his fingers at me. "Agreed?"

"Totally."

"All right, then we have a deal." My dad picked up his paper.

Mom handed me a lunch bag. It smelled like fresh cookies. "Go ahead." She kissed the top of my head. I jumped up and ran around the table to give my dad a big hug.

"Have a good day," he said, ruffling my hair.

"Try not be a spaz," Lucinda said. I stuck my tongue out at her. She stuck her tongue back out at me. We laughed. Sometimes my sister was okay.

twenty-five

Having a best friend is like:
- Fresh strawberries
- Clothes right out of the dryer
- Kittens asleep in the sunshine
- Finding money in your pocket
- The best thing ever

I ran to school. I couldn't have gone any faster even if I could fly. Finally I saw Katie up ahead just outside the gate to the playground.

"Wait!" I yelled out. Her eyes got really wide when she saw me. I ran up to her, but was panting so hard I couldn't say anything else for a minute.

"Is everything okay?"

"It's better than okay." I smiled. "My parents are

going to let me go to school here for the rest of the year!"

Katie squealed and we danced around together in a circle.

"We are going to have so much fun." Katie linked arms with me.

"That's not all. They're also letting me keep Winston."

Katie squealed again and we started dancing all over.

"Excuse me." Bethany pushed past us to get into the playground. She looked us up and down. "You're acting like you're still in first grade." A bunch of kids who were standing by the gate stopped to listen.

For a second I stopped dancing. I didn't want to look stupid. Bethany was Miranda's best friend, after all. What if everyone started laughing at me? Katie just laughed. She didn't care what Bethany thought. Then I realized I didn't really care either. People are people, and there isn't a right way or a wrong way to be.

"Why should we let the first graders have all the fun?" I asked. I started bouncing around, jumping in the air and turning circles. Katie laughed and started to dance around too.

"What's going on out here?" Grandma asked as she walked through the gate to school.

"Hi, Mrs. Doyle. We're celebrating what a great day it is," Katie said and she bounced in a circle around her.

"I told them only little kids act like that," Bethany said.

"You're never too old to celebrate having a good day," Grandma said with a wink. She leaned over and whispered in my ear. "Sometimes the best wishes take a while, but they're worth waiting for."

"They sure are."

Grandma clapped her hands. "All right everyone, time for school to start. Let's take this good day and keep it going inside."

Everyone began to gather their stuff and head for class. I couldn't believe it. I was going to a Humdrum school and not just for a week, but for the whole year. I felt like spinning around again.

"This is great," I said to Katie. "I couldn't have wished for things to go this well."

"You didn't need to wish for it. I wished it for you." Katie spun so her skirt swirled around.

School hadn't even started yet, and I already knew how to start my project for the fairy academy.

THINGS WE CAN LEARN FROM HUMDRUMS:
1. Always take the time to celebrate.
2. Friends always look out for each other.
3. The very best wishes are the ones you make for other people.

And it's only my second week at school. There's so much more to learn!

Find out what happens next in

Fourth Grade Fairy #2:
Wishes for Beginners

one

The most exciting thing that could ever happen to my fourth-grade class would be:

a. aliens from outer space come to suck us all up in their space ship and take us to their planet where they make us their rulers.

b. TV producers want to make a show about our class and we're all going to become famous. We'll wear giant sunglasses and carry our dogs around in handbags and everyone will want our autographs.

c. the president has selected our class to be his official kid advisors. We'll have fancy dinners at the White House while he asks us what we think needs to happen in the world. Personally, I plan to make sure he saves the polar bear.

d. none of the above.

. . . . .

I knew something really exciting *must* have happened because there was a big circle of people on the playground. Someone squealed and a couple of the girls were jumping up and down. T hey were bouncing all around like popcorn.

I saw my best friend Katie Hellegonds sitting on top of the slide. She liked to sit up there where she could see everything. I ran over to her. "What's going on?"

"I got a new book." Katie held it out. "It's all about NASA. My mom said it was for older kids, but I told her if I'm going to be an astronaut I couldn't read little kid books. Did you know there's no sound in space?" She didn't wait for me to answer. "The book is good, but I think it would be better with more pictures." She flipped through the pages.

I didn't always understand humans, or as we call them in the fairy community, humdrums. I come from a long line of fairy godmothers, but I always wanted to be just a plain humdrum. Or at least that was what I wanted until I learned how much fun being magical could be. After all, if I wasn't magical I wouldn't be able to talk to my dog, and have him talk back. Also, if I hadn't been magical I also wouldn't have been able to save my sister from being eaten by a lizard. It wasn't a large lizard or anything, my sister was really small at the time, sort of firefly-size. Even though it wasn't a giant, mutant lizard, the rescue plan still required me to be pretty clever. Not that I'm bragging or anything. I'd decided that I would stick with being magical and have a humdrum as a friend instead.

Until this school year I'd always attended the Cottingley Fairy Academy across town. I'd convinced my parents to let me study humdrums up close as long as no one figured out that I was a fairy. I'd only been going to Riverside Elementary for a couple of months. There were still a lot of things I didn't understand, but I was sure about this. No one in our class was excited that Katie had a book about rockets.

"Neat. It looks like a cool book." One tip for getting along with humdrums is that you should always act interested in things they're interested in, even if you aren't. For example, if your best friend has a pet bird you should pretend that you find it really fascinating that they clean themselves by having dust baths. (Even though taking a dust bath sounds like a stupid way to get clean.) "So, do you know why everyone else is so excited?" I asked trying to pull Katie's attention back.

Katie looked down at the cluster of girls. "Oh. Miranda's going to be in a wedding."

I watched Miranda's friend Bethany act like she was going to faint because she was so thrilled. Bethany has always been a drama queen, but even the other girls seemed excited. "Is it that big of a deal?"

Katie closed her book with a snap. "Exactly! Who cares that she gets to be a bridesmaid? If you ask, me a bunch of wedding cake doesn't make up for having to wear a fancy dress that itches and uncomfortable shoes."

My forehead wrinkled while I thought about it. I could think of a lot of things that sounded more fun than wearing uncomfortable shoes. However, my mom granted more wedding wishes than any other. Fairy godmothers spent a lot of time on romance, so there must be something to it.

"My dress is going to be light pink and we're going to carry bouquets of pink and white roses," I overheard Miranda say. The cluster of girls all sighed together.

"Roses mean true love," Bethany said. "Every flower has a meaning, you know." A few of the girls nodded. Bethany always had to be an expert on everything. "You have to be really careful about what you put in a wedding bouquet or you could doom the entire marriage."

I wasn't sure about the meaning of roses, but I was pretty sure Bethany was wrong about the part about the wrong flowers ruining things.

"I wonder what dandelions mean?" Paula asked.

Bethany ignored Paula.

"I'm not just some regular junior bridesmaid. I'm responsible for holding my cousin's bouquet during the wedding ceremony so she can concentrate on getting married." Miranda shrugged. "It's a pretty important job."

Everyone was silent for a moment as if they were awed by what Miranda would have to do. They were acting like she would be diffusing a bomb instead of holding a bunch of flowers. Humdrums were very confusing sometimes.

The bell rang. Katie jumped up and surfed down the slide, her arms out to keep her balance. I went down the ladder. If I tried to go down standing I would fall for sure, and if I sat down to slide, Bethany would make fun of me for acting like a kid. Fourth grade is really complicated. Sometimes it's okay to be a kid and other times everyone acts grown up. The hard part is figuring out which time you're supposed to act which way. It would be a lot easier if there were a rulebook. And so, part of my deal with my parents to attend humdrum school was that I had agreed to do presentations about humdrums to other sprites at the fairy academy. How was I supposed to help future fairy godmothers understand humdrums when I couldn't make sense of what they did half the time?

"I think it's cool you're going to be a junior bridesmaid," I said to Miranda as we lined up to go inside. "I'd love to see your dress sometime." Katie was my best friend, but I still couldn't help being fascinated by Miranda. It wasn't just me. Everyone in our entire school liked Miranda, including the really cranky lunch lady who would give her extra applesauce. Even the fifth graders liked Miranda and they spent most of their time ignoring the rest of us. I couldn't help thinking it would be really cool to have Miranda as a friend too.

"Do you think she's going to wear her bridesmaid dress to school?" Bethany asked. "Duh, Willow." She rolled her eyes at Paula.

I ignored Bethany. "Maybe you could bring in a picture of it."

"I should bring the picture of my cousin's dress. It is the most beautiful dress you've ever seen. It was on the cover of *Brides* magazine. It's strapless and the skirt has layers of lace and sort of swooshes down with all these beads and sequins on it."

All the girls around us gave another sigh of pleasure. I pulled my small humdrum notebook out of my bag and scribbled in it. *Dresses are better the more sparkle they have.* You never knew how humdrum information could be useful. Someday I might have to grant a dress wish and now I would know to add a bit of extra glitter.

Nathan, who was behind Miranda in line, snatched the notebook out of my hand and held it above his head. This wouldn't be a big deal except for the fact that he was the tallest person in our class. "Got your diary!" He yelled out.

"Give it back." I jumped up, trying to take it back from him, but I couldn't reach. He moved in a circle laughing.

"Who wants to hear Willow's secrets?" His friends laughed, which just encouraged him. "Dresses are better with more sparkle," he read out. "Aw, are you dreaming about your own wedding?"

My face was red hot. What if he flipped the pages and read the other things in there? I was pretty sure no one else in my class had to take notes on how to fit in.

I jumped up, but unless I could fly like my sister this was never going to work. "Please give it to me," I begged him. I looked around, hoping that our teacher, Ms. Caul, would come out and make him hand it over, but she was still inside. There's never a grown-up around when you want one.

Nathan cocked his head to the side. "Willow wants a wedding of her very own. Isn't that romantic?" He fluttered his eyelashes and put a sappy smile on his face. "She's in looooooove."

"Who is she going to find to marry *her*?" Bethany asked, and Nathan laughed.

Nathan held my notebook in the hand above his head as he tried to flip the pages to read more. "Maybe she says in here who she loves."

"Give it back," Katie demanded. Nathan laughed. Katie was even shorter than me. There was no way she was going to be able to grab the notebook. Unless there was a miracle, my life was about to be ruined. Nathan would read out all of my notes and everyone would make fun of me for the rest of the year. If my dog Winston was around I would make him run over and chew Nathan's lips off. He wouldn't do so much talking if he didn't have any lips.

Katie jabbed Nathan hard in the stomach. He gave a loud *oomph* and bent over. Katie grabbed the notebook out of his hand and gave it back to me.

"Hey, you aren't supposed to hit people," Bethany yelled out.

"Hey, you aren't supposed to steal things," Katie said with her hand on her hip, copying Bethany.

I clutched the notebook to my chest. I was never going to let it out of my hands again. I might ask my mom to enchant it so that if any humdrums ever got a hold of it again all it would show was pages with nothing on them other than *Nathan Filler is a big jerk*.

Ms. Caul came out and clapped her hands. "Okay everyone, we're supposed to be in a line."

I held my breath to see if Bethany would tell on Katie. Ms. Caul might want to look at my notebook to see what all the trouble was about. Even though I thought she was the best teacher in the whole world, and smelled like vanilla, I didn't want her to read it either. No one said anything; they shuffled back into a line so we could follow Ms. Caul into school.

"Willow is in wuuuve," Nathan whispered, making his voice sound like little kid. The entire line of fourth graders snickered.

I spun around and glared at him. He put his hand under his shirt and made his shirt pump in and out as if his heart was beating like crazy.

That was it. Nathan Filler was going to have to pay.

IF YOU ♥ THIS BOOK,
you'll love all the rest from

YOUR HOME AWAY FROM HOME:

AladdinMix.com

HERE YOU'LL GET:

- ♥ The first look at new releases

- ♥ Chapter excerpts from all the Aladdin M!X books

- ♥ Videos of your fave authors being interviewed

The Faeries' Promise

Read all the books in the series!

Read The Unicorn's Secret, the series that started it a

From Aladdin · Published by Simon & Schuster

Eileen Cook spent most of her teen years wishing she was someone else or somewhere else, which is great training for a writer. When she was unable to find any job postings for world famous author positions, she went to Michigan State University and became a counselor so she could at least support her book-buying habit. But real people have real problems, so she returned to writing. She liked having the ability to control the ending, which is much harder to do when you're a human.

Eileen lives in Vancouver with her husband and dogs and no longer wishes to be anyone or anywhere else. You can read more about Eileen, her books, and the things that strike her as funny at eileencook.com.